You need to leave that house of clocks.

Right now.

Don't wait for the clocks to stop...

For Jeremy, Jack and Ed

First published in the UK in 2020 by Usborne Publishing Ltd., Usborne House, 83-85 Saffron Hill, London EC1N 8RT, England, usborne.com.

Copyright © Ann-Marie Howell, 2020.

The right of Ann-Marie Howell to be identified as the author of this work has been asserted by her in accordance with the Copyright, Designs and Patents Act, 1988.

Cover, inside illustrations and map by Saara Katariina Söderlund © Usborne Publishing, 2020.

Photo of Ann-Marie Howell © Nick Ilott Photography, 2019.

The name Usborne and the devices ♈ ⊕ are Trade Marks of Usborne Publishing Ltd.

A CIP catalogue record for this book is available from the British Library.

JFMAMJJASON /19   05232/1   ISBN: 9781474959568

Printed and bound in Great Britain by CPI Group (UK) Ltd, Croydon, CR0 4YY.

# Contents

# The HOUSE of ONE HUNDRED CLOCKS

## A. M. HOWELL

USBORNE

# CAMBRIDGE, 1905

Marchington & Sons

University Arms Hotel

STREET

DOWNING STREET

GONVILLE PLACE

PARKER'S PIECE

Mr Westcott's house

LENSFIELD ROAD

TRUMPINGTON STREET

Peterhouse College

# CHAPTER I

# The Contract

Helena grasped the bars of the domed birdcage resting on her lap until her fingers ached. Mr Westcott was staring into the cage with an odd kind of intent that danced a shiver across the back of her neck. His rake-thin frame leaned forward across the desk, his eyes narrowing. "You omitted to say in your acceptance letter that you were bringing...a...bird," he said, his sallow cheeks tightening as he glanced first at Helena's father, and then at Helena.

Mr Westcott's sister stood beside him in a high-waisted silk dress the colour of peaches, her gloved hand resting on the back of his chair. They had the same small sapphire blue eyes. Miss Westcott's eyes were crinkling into a smile as they looked at Helena. Mr Westcott's were not.

Helena's skin bristled as she glanced at her father, who was sitting bolt upright in his chair, his shoulders taut.

"Jack and Jill went up the hill. Pail of water. *Snicker-squawk!*"

Mr Westcott's forehead furrowed at the bird.

"Shush," Helena murmured, reaching through the brass bars and running a finger down her parrot's shimmery green-blue tail feathers. Mr Westcott had called her mother's parrot "a bird". Except he wasn't just any old bird. Orbit was a Blue-fronted Amazon. It was important Mr Westcott knew that, but Helena sensed now was not quite the right time to give him a lesson on exotic creatures.

Miss Westcott's eyes twinkled. "What an amusing parrot," she said in a sing-song voice.

The knot in Helena's stomach unwound a little and she returned the woman's warm smile. Amongst the wood panelling, papers and books in the study, Miss Westcott's smile really was quite dazzling. When she looked Helena in the eye, it made her wish she had worn her best navy coat, the one with the blue silk buttons. Helena tugged at the almost too-small sleeves of her beige cotton jacket, that her father had said would be more suitable for a stay in Cambridge during what was turning out to be a rather cool and disappointing June.

"My sincere apologies, Mr Westcott. And to you too, Miss Westcott," Helena's father said, throwing Helena a look which she interpreted to mean, *Keep that parrot quiet or else.* He pulled at his close-clipped beard. "There was so little time, and you made it clear in your correspondence that you were in urgent need of a timekeeper and clock conservator. Wherever my daughter Helena goes, her parrot goes too."

Mr Westcott stood up to turn and face a large window, which overlooked Trumpington Street and beyond, to a tapestry of colour blooming behind the railed gardens of a university college. He folded his arms and a small huff expelled from his mouth. Noises from outside carried through the glass. A horse and cart rumbling. The pounding of children's footsteps and peals of laughter. Bicycle bells clamouring. Helena closed her eyes for little more than a blink – long enough to imagine herself outside in the fresh air and out of the oppressive wooden room, where everything seemed dull and dusty.

"Oh, brother dearest," Miss Westcott said lightly. "What harm will a parrot do?"

"I don't have quite the same…affinity with birds as you do, Katherine," said Mr Westcott, turning to give her a sharp look. There was something in the tone of his voice that implied his words meant something different to his sister. He paused. "Very well," he said curtly. "But the bird must stay in its cage. It must not be allowed to fly in the house or it will damage the clocks." His face had been pale when they had arrived. Now his skin was almost translucent, like a vampire or an animal which only ventured out at night.

Helena frowned. Mr Westcott did not seem too fond of birds, but at least his sister was a trifle more amenable. Memories of Orbit's arrival four years ago sprang into her head. Father had gladly spent more than a month's wages on the parrot as a birthday present for her mother, after she had become besotted with his chattering in the aviary of a local pet shop they used to pass on their way home from school. The shopkeeper had suggested a fancier (and more expensive) parrot with golden plumage, but Mother would not be dissuaded. "Thank you, sir, but I do not desire this parrot for his looks, it is his voice and personality that amuses me. I have a feeling he will be the perfect addition to our small family," her mother had said with a broad smile. And she had been right.

"My parrot's name is Orbit," Helena said. The words popped out of her mouth before she even had a chance to realize she was thinking them. Mother used to say that was one of her most endearing (and troublesome) qualities – her ability to speak without first thinking of the consequences. The narrowing of Mr Westcott's eyes seemed to suggest he might not agree with the endearing part. Helena sank into her chair, its wooden engravings digging into her back.

"What an interesting name for a bird," Katherine Westcott said, giving Helena another sunny smile. "I should like to be introduced to Orbit…at an appropriate time of course." She glanced at her brother.

A sudden tinkling chime burst from a silver carriage clock, standing on Mr Westcott's desk, to mark quarter to the hour. The noise reminded Helena of a gentle waterfall. Chimes from other rooms in the house began to bleed through the wooden walls. High-pitched ones, deep ones, silvery toned and soaring ones. Orbit squawked and screeched in his cage, his pupils wide and dilated. Helena swallowed, gripped the cage bars more tightly. How many clocks did Mr Westcott have exactly?

"This clock conservator position is extremely well-paid, Helena," her father had said the previous week, his eyes shinier than they had been for a while. "Board and lodgings are provided, so I'll be able to save every pound and shilling for a clock-making shop of our own. And Cambridge is a beautiful town, by all accounts. I think perhaps it will be good for us – to be somewhere new."

"But I want to stay in London," Helena had replied, glancing around the small parlour of their suburban terraced house, and pausing at the portrait of herself, Father and Mother, which had been painted two years earlier, in 1903 when Helena was ten. Mother's round face was rosebud healthy, there was no sign of the terrible sickness which would sweep through their front door and out again, taking Mother with it. "All of our things are here. All of *Mother's* things are here."

"Pop goes the weasel. Mother, Mother, Mother," Orbit had squawked, walking along the back of the armchair until he reached Helena's shoulder. He'd nuzzled his beak into her hair and tugged on a few chestnut-brown strands until her scalp began to smart. She'd picked Orbit up and placed him on her lap. The bird was still pining, and Mother had been gone almost twelve months now.

"I have committed to the position for as long as Mr Westcott requires my assistance, but it will not be for ever. Our house and all of our things will still be here when we get back," Helena's father had said firmly, drawing the conversation to a close in the same way he drew the curtains at night, and Helena knew there would be no further discussion.

Helena felt a renewed unease at the open-ended nature of their stay, as Mr Westcott's eyes flickered to her and Orbit and back again.

"You understand the terms of the contract, Mr Graham?" Mr Westcott asked. His Adam's apple bobbed in his scrawny throat. "I do believe you were sent them in advance of your arrival."

Helena scrunched up her nose. What did Mr Westcott mean by "terms"?

"Yes," Helena's father replied, his eyebrows knitting together. He glanced at Helena and swallowed.

Mr Westcott opened a folder, pulled out a stiff piece of paper and slid it across the large desk past an engraved, brass telephone with a wooden mouthpiece, which Helena had seen her father give frequent appraising glances. It made Helena realize just how rich Mr Westcott must be, for she did not know anyone who could afford to have a telephone in their own home. His fingers lingered on the edge of the contract for a second, as if he was hesitant to part with it.

Helena leaned forward to better see the words. The creamy parchment was covered in small swirly writing.

*Worldly possessions…*

*Signed over…*

*Damaged…*

*If a single clock should stop…*

Helena sucked in a breath.

Mr Westcott and his sister peered at her.

Her father ignored her, picked up a pen, dipped it in a pot of black ink and scribbled his signature on the bottom of the paper.

"It is important my clock collection is maintained and kept in good working order at all times," said Mr Westcott.

Helena stared at their host, who was now looking at a gloomy long-ago family portrait of a gentleman and lady with two children, standing next to a huge longcase clock. He sniffed, ran a finger under his nose. "No clock must be allowed to stop – ever. You do realize the consequence of that?"

"Father?" Helena said, her voice so small that if it had been an object it would have slid between the gaps in the floorboards. There was something unsaid in this room, something that made her feel rather cold.

"Father, Father. Three blind mice," Orbit squawked.

"I don't understand," said Helena, the metal cage suddenly feeling like a lead weight on her lap. "Why must no clock stop?"

"Not now, Helena," her father said in a firm voice, sliding the signed paper back across the table to Mr Westcott.

"Oh, my dear girl," Katherine Westcott said. It was then that Helena noticed the white combs lined with tiny baby-blue feathers holding her silky dark hair in place. "There is no need for you to worry."

Helena's father cleared his throat, turned to look at her. "It is my job to wind the clocks – keep them ticking, make sure they are in fine working order. If any one of them stops or is damaged, in any way…then we will hand over…all of our possessions as recompense."

Helena's throat tightened into a knot.

"*Snicker, snicker, snicker,*" Orbit chirped, bobbing his head.

"We have to give away our things if any of the clocks stop or are damaged?" Helena's breathing was jerky, and she struggled to pull air into her lungs. "But why?"

"Clocks, clocks, clocks. Dickory, dockery clocks," squawked Orbit loudly.

The look Helena's father gave Mr Westcott and his sister was one which requested help.

But it seemed neither Mr Westcott nor Katherine Westcott had help to give. Or maybe they had some but were not in the right frames of mind to dispense it, at that moment.

Helena gave Katherine Westcott what she hoped was a beseeching look.

"That is correct," Katherine Westcott said eventually, picking up the signed contract. A gentle flush stained her cheeks. "The contract is a…deterrent. So that my brother can be certain that any clock conservator he employs will fulfil the requirements of the post and not let any clock stop." She paused, her gaze settling on Helena's father. "Oh, and Mr Graham, it is imperative that this arrangement is kept as a private matter. You may witness some unexpected things in this house and anything you or Helena hear or see must never be spoken of, even amongst yourselves." Katherine Westcott held the contract close to her chest. "Otherwise, the terms will be initiated and again, you will forfeit the right to all of your possessions." She gave them both what Helena interpreted to be an apologetic look.

Mr Westcott's jaw tensed as he looked up at his sister, then away again.

Helena blinked, forcing the words into some sort of order in her head. But they would not settle or make any sense. And her question seemed to float unanswered.

Mr Westcott's gaze settled on Orbit's golden cage. There was an odd, feverish gleam in his eyes.

Helena curled her arms around the cage, a tree of panic sprouting in her stomach. She had been forced to move from their perfectly pleasant home in the London suburbs to this strange, stuffy house and now this? If a single clock stopped they would lose all of their things, including the one most irreplaceable and precious thing Helena must not lose at any cost. And, stranger still was that everything inside the house was never to be spoken of… *What had her father agreed to?*

# CHAPTER 2

# Stanley Richards

"I am terribly sorry about the terms of the contract," said Miss Westcott, who had asked them to call her Katherine. She led them from Mr Westcott's study and Helena heard the door being locked behind them. "My brother has been troubled since his wife left eight months ago." She brought a hand to her throat, as if it pained her to say this. "He cares for his clocks deeply. More than...well...anything really." She paused, shaking her delicate head sadly. Rearranging her face into something a little brighter, she tugged at a bell pull on the wall.

Helena heard a distant ring, followed by footsteps thumping up the stairs.

"Stanley will show you to your rooms," Katherine said, "and explain the workings of the house." She pulled an enamel-fronted pocket watch from her small purse, glanced at it and frowned. "I have another appointment, so need to leave, I'm afraid. However, I do visit every evening for the clock inspections." She put her watch away and bent down, looked Helena in the eye. Her perfume, cloud-like and heady, reminded Helena of walks in flower-filled gardens. "I shall look forward to becoming properly acquainted with your lovely parrot another time, Helena," she said.

Helena managed to give her a wide smile. "I shall look forward to it too."

With little more than a nod, Katherine Westcott swept out of the house in a flurry of bustling skirts. Helena had a sudden urge to follow her. As their train from London had chugged its way through the low-lying East Anglian countryside earlier that day, Helena had pressed her father for more details about Mr Westcott and the house where they would be staying.

"Mr Westcott is one of the wealthiest men in the East of England. His family made money investing in printing presses and newspapers. He has one of the grandest town houses in the whole of Cambridge, by all accounts, and we will stay as his guests while I work on the clocks," her father said, his box of clockmaker's tools (which he refused to place in the overhead compartment in case it got damaged) wobbling on his knees.

"Does he have a wife? Children?" asked Helena, hoping there might at least be someone she could befriend in the house.

"There has been no mention of either," replied her father. "He does have a sister though – Katherine – who is most concerned for his welfare, wishes to ensure his clock collection is kept in fine working order. She is visiting from London but staying elsewhere. Mr Westcott values his privacy by all accounts."

Helena's mood had lightened a little. Even without children to play with, perhaps a Cambridge town house with delicious food and beautiful furnishings wouldn't be too dreadful. The start to the summer in London had been a damp one, with raincoats required for even the shortest of walks and the fire in the parlour lit nightly. Helena hoped that in Cambridge the current chill would be swallowed up by sunny days and birdsong. In between her father looking after the clocks, she imagined walks with him, exploring untamed riverbanks full of darting dragonflies, or having lengthy afternoon teas and delicious jam-filled cakes, watching boaters and students larking about. Perhaps it would be the change her father needed to make him remember the things they had used to do together, before their lives had changed so horribly and he had decided to squirrel himself away in his clockmaker's workshop for hours on end.

But all thoughts of birdsong and greenery and exploring a new town were squashed under the floorboards as Helena began to understand the terms of the task her father had accepted. *How could he agree that their possessions would be taken if the clocks stopped? And how many clocks was her father to be responsible for exactly?* She glanced around, counting more than twelve in the hallway alone.

With the front door firmly shut and Katherine gone, a stocky young man – perhaps no more than eighteen years old – in a tweed suit came thundering down the hallway. His smile caused his cheeks to firm into round apples. His eyes widened at the sight of Orbit in his cage next to Helena's feet. "What a fine parrot. Male or female?"

"Male," Helena replied in a small voice. "At least we think so. It's often difficult to tell with parrots."

"Does he speak?" said the young man.

"Yes, he does rather," Helena said, her shoulders relaxing a little.

"Hickory-dickory…" Orbit croaked.

"How wonderful!" the young man said in delight. "Oh, I should introduce myself. I'm Stanley Richards, but please do call me Stanley. I work for the Westcott family." He stuck out his hand.

Helena stared at it. Was he expecting her to shake his hand? He wasn't wearing gloves and his fingertips were stained with ink and something that looked a little like chalk. Occasionally Helena had accompanied her father on house visits while he conserved expensive clocks in the smarter parts of London, like Chelsea and Kensington. There, the servants were black-suited and white-gloved, and you placed your calling card on a silver tray to announce your arrival. There was never any question of shaking hands with the staff and calling them by their first name. Stanley looked at her expectantly, gave her a bright smile, which brought a smile to Helena's lips in return. Maybe things were done differently here in Cambridge. She held out her hand and Stanley shook it firmly, leaving a white powdery residue on her palm.

"And you must be Mr Graham," Stanley said, turning to Helena's father. "Welcome to Mr Westcott's home."

Helena glanced around the large hallway and wiped her chalky palm on her jacket. It did not seem like a home. Where were the fancy silk-covered chairs, the tall vases filled with sweet-scented flowers, the rugs? Where was the cosy fire crackling in the grate, to take the edge off the early evening coolness? There was nothing here that made the building into a home.

Six dark-wood longcase clocks lined each wall of the wide hallway. They were tall, the ornament-like finials on their hoods almost touching the ceiling. Their pendulums swung rhythmically through small, round lenticular viewing windows like waving hands. At the end of the hall, in front of the cold and yawning fireplace, was a table bearing the weight of a large four-tier, gold pagoda clock, which reminded Helena of a wedding cake. It was emitting a fast tick-tick-tick that made her feel quite breathless. To the right and left were two smaller tables on top of which huddled a few smaller silver and gold carriage clocks. Helena stared at the ghostly imprints on the walls where paintings had once hung, as ticks and tocks and clicks echoed around them. Her father hadn't brought her to stay in a grand house, he had brought her to a museum crammed to the rafters with clocks.

Helena picked up Orbit's cage and held it close to her chest as Stanley led them to the stairs, their travelling trunk in his arms. She clenched her jaw and focused on the heels of Stanley's black shoes. Her eyes smarted. How could her father have promised to come and work here with no end date for their return to London? The way Mr Westcott's snaky eyes had looked at Orbit sent a shiver down the back of her legs. And the contract he had signed! His sister did not seem too impressed with the arrangement, but there was probably little she could do to persuade him to behave differently.

"What a fine collection of clocks," Helena's father murmured as they traipsed upstairs.

Stanley paused on the first-floor landing, wincing as he shifted their heavy trunk. "Yes, Mr Graham. I think there are about one hundred of them. Longcase clocks, carriage clocks, skeleton clocks and that's not counting the pocket watches."

"Clocks, clocks, clocks," piped up Orbit.

"Why did the last clock conservator leave?" asked

her father. "I posed the question to Mr Westcott in my correspondence, but did not receive a reply."

"I'm afraid Mr Westcott doesn't include me in such discussions," Stanley replied with a small shrug.

Helena's father gave Stanley a firm smile. "Well then. You had better show us to our rooms, so I can make a start."

"What, tonight?" exclaimed Helena. It was almost six o'clock and she was hoping for nothing more than a light supper (and some fruit for Orbit) and a comfortable bed after their journey.

"But of course, Helena. There is no time to waste. I need to make an inventory of the clocks, check their condition, see which ones need winding," said her father.

"Of course, Mr Graham," said Stanley continuing up the grand-looking staircase, where ornately carved vines entwined the wooden bannister. He paused, flashed them both a bright smile. "I must say, it's jolly nice to have you both staying here."

Stanley's friendly welcome caused Helena to stifle a small smile of her own, annoyed that her lips could think that smiling at a time like this was a good idea at all. It wasn't nice at all. It was actually the very worst of days and she could not wait until she was alone with her father so she could make her opinions better known.

Stanley looked up at a large longcase clock, which was emitting a low-level tock. "Oh dear," he said with a sigh, placing the trunk on the floor with a thump. "Please get ready. The clocks are about to strike the hour."

Helena and her father exchanged a glance.

They watched as Stanley gave them both an apologetic grimace and clamped his hands to his ears.

Helena glanced again at her father, whose wrinkled forehead indicated he felt as perplexed as she did. Things in this house were just becoming odder and odder by the minute.

# CHAPTER 3

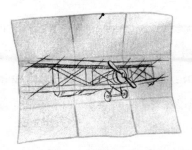

# Flying Machine

The first loud dong came from the clock they were standing next to. Orbit squawked and flapped his wings against the cage bars.

The second, third and fourth dongs drifted up the stairs from behind like smoke.

The fifth and sixth were urgent and high-pitched and came from the floor above.

Then there were too many to count.

Deep dongs and high, flighty chimes.

Cuckoo clocks chirping.

Tinny, plinky-plonk music like the wind-up musical

box her father had made for Helena one Christmas.

Stanley had his hands clamped over his ears, his eyes squeezed shut as if the noise pained him.

Helena's father's jaw dropped open, his head tilted to the cacophony of sounds as if he was examining each in turn. "They are not all striking in time with one another," he said above the noise. "That must be rectified at once."

Orbit lurched from side to side in his cage. "*Ding-dong-tick-tock*-clocks," he yelled, his beady eyes wide and scared. "Mother, Mother, Mother!"

"Shush. It's okay, Orbit," Helena soothed, even though she felt far from okay.

The last loud "dong" came from the floor above, deeper and grander than all the rest, as if saying "enough".

Stanley opened his eyes and sighed. Then, as if nothing out of the ordinary had happened, he hoisted their trunk into his arms once more and made his way up the second and third flights of stairs, gesturing for Helena and her father to follow.

"Well," said Helena's father. His eyes were bright, his cheeks flushed as he clutched his toolbox.

Helena was familiar with this particular look. It was

often etched on his face when she arrived after school at the clockmaker's workshop he shared with two other men. His head would be bent over a gold pocket watch, or an elegant brass carriage clock. "You see this, Helena?" he would say. "This is one of the finest timepieces a person could own. Do you see the springs? The porcelain face? The way it keeps the time? Isn't it wonderful that such an object was imagined and invented!" Helena would smile and wait for her father to finish his latest task, all the while trying to remember the last time he had spoken about *her* in such an affectionate way.

At the very top of the house a small landing opened onto corridors to the left and right. It was gloomier up here, the windows smaller, the walls painted rather than papered, the wooden skirting boards scuffed.

"Mr Westcott's rooms are along the corridor to the left," Stanley said. "Your rooms are to the right."

"Mr Westcott sleeps in the…servants' quarters?" Helena's father said in surprise.

Stanley shrugged. "The clocks occupy all of the other rooms."

"*All* of them?" Helena said, her eyes widening.

"Every. Single. One," Stanley said with a heavy sigh.

A window on the landing was open and a breath of air curled around Helena's neck. A noise, like paper fluttering in a breeze, tickled her ears. Stanley and her father appeared not to have heard it, so busy were they talking about mealtimes and the running of the house as they made their way down the corridor to the right. Helena glanced in the direction of the sound. There – pinned to the wall just above head height at the entrance to the other corridor.

It was a drawing, but she was too far away to see what it was. Placing Orbit's cage down, she darted across the landing and stood on tiptoes to look at the picture. Lines and angles and wings. It was a detailed pencil drawing of a flying machine. She traced a finger along the line of a wing, thought about the photographs she had seen in the *London Herald* newspaper of the Wright brothers' machine. This drawing was almost identical.

A slim hand reached above Helena's head and pulled the paper from the wall. The pin fell to the floor. Stanley's eyes narrowed as he looked at the drawing, then he carefully folded it three times and pushed it into his jacket pocket.

"I'm sorry," Helena said, her face feeling warm. "It was on the wall and I wondered…"

"Wondering is good," Stanley said softly.

Helena looked at him blankly. Whatever did he mean?

Stanley pulled out an ink-stained handkerchief and wiped his forehead. "I really am pleased you and your father have come to stay." As he turned to walk away, he paused, looked back. "If you happen to see other drawings pinned to the walls, please let me know and I'll remove them."

Helena remembered Katherine's instructions not to speak of anything they heard or saw in the house. Should she do as Stanley asked? She blinked, her head spinning a little. The multitude of striking clocks. The new house. Drawings pinned to walls. She suddenly felt untethered, as if she herself was in one of the Wright brothers' great flying machines, taking off on a journey somewhere unknown, and she didn't like it one little bit.

# CHAPTER 4

# Questions

Helena's thoughts rolled around in her head like marbles as she and her father explored their new accommodation in the servants' quarters of the town house. "Why did you agree to Mr Westcott's demands?" she asked her father hotly, now that they were alone. Her room was sparsely furnished – a single bed with a pink bedspread, a chest of drawers beside it and a window overlooking Trumpington Street. There was an even more impressive view of the university college from up here, the assortment of buff stone and red-brick buildings giving off an air of quiet importance.

Father unpacked their leather trunk, passing Helena a bundle of summer day dresses, skirts and blouses (badly folded and creased) and two well-worn knitted cardigans with patches on the elbows.

"I just don't understand," Helena persisted, depositing the clothes unceremoniously on the bed. "Why would you promise that horrid man all of our things? Why must the clocks not stop?"

Helena's father lifted his head. "It is not for us to question the decisions of others," he said firmly.

"It is when we could lose everything," Helena said, anger wobbling her voice. "Did you see the way Mr Westcott looked at Orbit? He was like…a lion about to pounce on a zebra! If the clocks stop, he will take him from us."

Helena's father sat back on his heels and barked out a laugh. "My dear, do not worry. Orbit is safe, as are all of our things. Mr Westcott is one of the wealthiest men in the region, if not the country. He could afford to buy one thousand parrots if he so wished. This is an opportunity for us, Helena. It is a chance for us to try and move forward with our lives."

Helena's eyes dropped to the floor. She knew they had to move forward. But the very act of moving away from the past seemed to mean it was closer to being forgotten.

"This clock contract is rather unusual, but I am almost certain it would be null and void if looked over by a solicitor. But there is no need for us to waste precious expense having it examined, for I shall work on the clocks and they will not stop. You have nothing to worry about," her father said, taking out the last of her clothes from the trunk and closing it.

Helena sat on the edge of the bed and picked at a loose thread on the bedspread.

"Jack and Jill. Pail of water. *Squawk!*" said Orbit, pecking at the cage bars.

Helena's father perched on the bed beside her. "I know Mr Westcott appears slightly…eccentric. And that some of his ideas are a little peculiar. But there really is no need to worry. We will keep the clocks ticking and make a small fortune during the time we are here. This will change our lives, Helena…imagine, one day, a clockmaker's workshop of our own," he said, his lips tilting into a smile. "My good friend Mr Smith, who owns a clock factory in Clerkenwell, says he will help me locate a suitable property in the city. It will be a fresh start for us all when we return to London."

"But why does Mr Westcott collect all of these clocks? And he lives in the servants' quarters – isn't that a little unusual?"

Her father sighed. "That is enough now, Helena. No more questions please – it is important we are not intrusive and impolite while we are here. Tomorrow morning I will need you to assist me. There are more clocks in Mr Westcott's collection than I thought – and I fear I shall need some help. The longcase clocks will need winding every eight days. The smaller clocks and watches will need attention every day or so. We need a comprehensive list of what needs doing and when." And just like a pail of water being poured over a flickering flame, their conversation was extinguished.

Helena's father stored the empty trunk under her bed and returned to his own room for his notebook and tools. "I must go and examine at least one room of clocks before we have supper, discover what our work will entail," he said, so distracted that he closed the door behind him without even saying goodbye.

"Hickory-dickory clocks," Orbit snickered, bending to pull a sunflower seed from his brass pot and nibbling on it.

Helena poked a finger through the cage bars and stroked his blue-green tail feathers.

"Mother-Mother-Mother," Orbit cawed (somewhat hopefully Helena thought).

Helena bit down on her bottom lip, glanced at the door. She heard the sound of her father's footsteps thudding down the landing towards the stairs. "Mother loves Helena. Mother loves Helena," she whispered to the parrot. Orbit regarded her for a second and ruffled his neck feathers. "Mother loves Helena. Mother loves Helena," she repeated softly.

"Mother-loves-Helena-Mother-loves-Helena, hickory-dickory *squawk*!" Orbit replied, swaying from side to side in time to the words he had been taught.

His voice and words sent an arrow into Helena's chest and tears smarted her eyes. She knew she was foolish. Coaxing Orbit to repeat phrases that her mother had lovingly spent hours teaching him was like prodding an open wound. But she must not let Orbit forget. When he spoke, it brought back clear-as-day memories of the parrot standing proudly on the arm of the easy chair in the parlour, while her mother smiled and cajoled and taught her bird to talk and sing nursery rhymes. "I sometimes feel like this beautiful parrot is part of my own being," her mother would say softly, feeding Orbit slices of apple as he nuzzled her palm.

Helena sat back on her heels and rubbed her weary eyes. She was trying her best to move on, as Father was so clearly managing to do. But how could she fully do that when she was terrified of Orbit forgetting everything Mother had taught him? It would be like losing Mother all over again and that would be just too hard to bear.

Just after six-thirty that evening, Helena covered Orbit's cage with his brown and green patchwork night cloth (*To remind him of the treetops*, Mother had said as she'd stitched it together) and re-traced her steps downstairs. A smell wound its way upwards that made her stomach growl. She paused and sniffed. Something fresh and light. At least Mr Westcott employed a decent cook – that would make their stay a little more bearable. She paused on the second floor and peered round each half-opened door. Stanley had not been exaggerating when he said clocks occupied every room in the house. Her eyes widened at rooms that had been stripped of their furnishings and the sounds of the ticks and tocks and clicks and clunks of the clocks, which had replaced them. Lantern clocks (which looked like their name); tables loaded with carriage clocks (small and box-like with a carrying handle on top); skeleton clocks (with a glass dome cover so their cogs and springs and working mechanisms were visible to all) and table clocks (which had short pendulums, allowing them to stand on a surface). And overshadowing them all was the enormous collection of longcases, which, judging by their number, seemed to be Mr Westcott's favourite type of clock. They were like free-standing towers, long pendulums swinging in the main bodies of the cases, their hoods enclosing the clock faces.

Helena walked into a room of eight longcase clocks. Purple wisteria-patterned wallpaper peeked out between them. She supposed the room had once been a bedroom, a very fine one by the looks of things. Helena paused in front of each clock. Their dark wooden cases were polished to a high shine. The outsides of the clocks were well cared for, that much was apparent. The pendulums were all swinging in different rhythms, the tick-tocks spilling over each other into a muddle of noise. The largest in the room was a clock with an ordinary brass face, but above it was an arched dial, which rotated to show the phases of the moon. Except the two painted moons were not like the one in the sky, they were grotesque childish faces with too-close-together piggy eyes, rouged cheeks and pursed, rosebud lips. The same face had been painted onto the pendulum bob, which swung back and forth through the lenticular window, as if it was playing an eerie game of peek-a-boo. It was hypnotic and horrible at the same time. Helena shivered. Why had Mr Westcott filled a bedroom full to bursting with mechanical things? She was no stranger to the idea of obsession. Her father loved his work with a passion that had only increased since her mother died. This did not anger Helena, more caused a ball of disbelief to sit heavy in her stomach. It was plain to her that he loved things made out of wood and metal more than his own flesh and blood family. Maybe that was why her father seemed so sympathetic to Mr Westcott's demands?

"Oh, here you are," her father said, his footsteps echoing over the bare wooden boards. "Outstanding! Look at this clock, Helena," he said gazing at the one nearest the door. "It is very rare – from Germany. It would have cost a small fortune. And this next to it – see how the wooden casing at the sides has been replaced with glass so it displays the workings? Look at the cogs and gears. See how the pendulum regulates the force of the weight?"

Helena shook her head and sighed, a familiar feeling of boredom at hearing such details settling over her. She looked at the chair by the door, which faced into the room. Perhaps this was where Mr Westcott sat to admire his clock collection.

Helena wandered to one of the two large windows and noticed a group of young women in beautiful gauzy white dresses who were arriving at the university college in hansom cabs, their hair pulled into elaborate and sophisticated twists and topknots.

"Look, Father," she said.

Her father joined her at the window. "Ah-ha," he said with a smile, as they watched the women laughing and adjusting their shawls. "I have a clock-making acquaintance whose father attended Cambridge University. He told me great tales of their escapades in May Week."

"May Week? But it's June," said Helena wrinkling her nose.

"May Week marks the end of the students' exams; it's a time for celebration. The university colleges – like the one across the street, which I believe is called

Peterhouse – hold balls, extravagant parties, that continue until dawn," said her father. "It's odd that May Week takes place in June, I have no idea why."

"Good evening, Helena, Mr Graham," interrupted a voice. Stanley was standing in the doorway. "Supper is ready."

Helena smiled. "Thank you," she said, glancing at her father, who had become distracted by a clock with gleaming golden finials on its hood.

"Where is your parrot?" Stanley asked.

"In…my room," Helena replied.

"He must be lonely. Bring him downstairs and he can join us for supper," said Stanley.

Helena's cheeks stretched into a smile. "Are you certain? Mr Westcott said he must stay in the cage."

"Your parrot can't do any harm in the kitchen," Stanley said with a grin.

Helena's smile broadened. Racing back upstairs, she pulled open her bedroom door. She paused, blinked. The night cloth covering Orbit's cage had been removed and was neatly folded on her pillow. She slowly walked to it and picked it up, her eyes warily scanning the room. Nothing else had changed. Her small silver pocket watch was ticking on the chest of drawers. The clothes she had flung on the bed earlier still lay in a messy jumble.

A tapping sound was coming from inside the cage. Helena kneeled, her heart thumping a little harder than usual. Orbit was contentedly pecking at something that had been tied to the bars. Something that had most certainly not been there when she had left him.

# Chapter 5

# The Mirror

An icy-breathed shiver goosebumped the skin on Helena's arms. She grasped the bars of Orbit's cage and stared at the small oval mirror, which had been attached to it with a buttery yellow ribbon. She pulled on the ribbon. It was silky and expensive looking. The mirror was gilt-edged and perfectly rounded in her palm, as if it had been designed for a bird's cage. She held it up to her face, the puzzlement in her hazel eyes reflecting back at her. *Who had put it there?* Reattaching the mirror (to Orbit's delight), she leaped to her feet, strode to the door and peered down the corridor. The electric wall lights flickered and hissed, throwing wobbly shadows onto the floorboards. They did not have electric lamps at home, still relying on the gas lamps that Mother had hated with a passion, due to the frequent black deposits they left on the furnishings and walls. Perhaps electricity was not the advance into modernity that people claimed it to be, for she had heard a terrible tale of a family who threw a cushion at their new spark-spitting electric lamp, only for the fabric to catch alight and the entire room go up in flames.

"Hello?" Helena called, giving the hissing lights an anxious glance and stepping away from them. "Is anyone there?"

A floorboard creaked at the end of the corridor near the stairs, just out of sight. Her skin prickled and her feet seemed to weld themselves to the floor. The clocks began to strike and chime and clamour on the floors below. It was seven o'clock already. Time had slipped by unnoticed.

"Hello, Mother. Hello, Mother. Hello, Mother," Orbit squawked, his voice making Helena's insides dissolve into jelly. That was how Orbit used to greet Mother when she entered the room.

*Ding-ding-ding-ding.*

*Bong-bong-bong-bong-bong.*

*Ting-ting-ting-ting.*

She was being watched, she was certain of it. "Hello?" she called again, but her voice was swallowed up by the strikes of the clocks. The shadows at the end of the hallway began to move, turn and evolve into a person-like shape. Helena curled her fingers into her sweaty palms, her heart ricocheting around her chest. A final loud "dong" from the floor below marked the end of the clocks striking. There was another creak and flicker of the wall lights.

"Helena, whatever is keeping you? Stanley is waiting." Her father. Standing with his hands on his hips at the top of the stairs, a frown knitting his bushy eyebrows together.

Helena let out a long, slow breath. The house's clocks and shadows were seeping under her skin, causing her to imagine people who weren't there. She glanced back into her room. But she had not imagined the mysterious new addition to Orbit's cage. She wondered if she should tell her father of the discovery, but he had already gone, his footsteps retreating hurriedly down the stairs.

The scent Helena had smelled earlier grew stronger as she followed her father down the final set of stairs to the basement kitchen. It was a large room, mirroring the entire footprint of the house above.

"Welcome," said Stanley, gesturing for them to take a seat at the table.

Helena blinked. Over his shirt (with its sleeves rolled up) and trousers, Stanley was wearing an apron.

"Um…thank you," her father said, giving Helena a worried glance.

Helena looked around for the cook, for surely Mr Westcott should have an army of servants to help in his grand house with its electric lights, telephone and myriad of clocks? She wondered if the cook had stepped outside, as she watched tendrils of steam rising from a copper pot gently bubbling on the range. Cooking was not a strong point for either Helena or her father. While Father said they could not afford regular help in the home, he did pay Mrs Partridge next door to provide them with one hot meal a day. But the meat stews were often gristly (and not very meaty) and rice puddings lumpy and needing to be forced down with lashings of milk. Helena supposed in a way she was lucky that her father did not expect her to take on the role of woman of the house – for that is what had happened to her friend Jane when her mother had died. She sometimes saw Jane at the school gates with her younger brothers, a shopping basket swinging from an arm and a resigned look on her face, at the way her life had upended and jolted her into a position of responsibility she was not ready for.

Four places were laid at the farmhouse table, which could easily have seated ten people. Helena frowned. Where were the place settings for the chambermaids, the housekeeper and the cook?

"You can put your parrot's cage on that chair if you like. I take it he likes fruit?" said Stanley, gesturing to a chair. On the table in front of the chair sat a plate of apple slices arranged in a wheel shape. Stanley was a very thoughtful man indeed.

"I've made some asparagus soup." Stanley paused, swallowed. "And fried eels. I must admit, it is the first time I've made this dish, but Mrs Beeton says…"

"Oh…Mrs Beeton –" said Helena's father, looking around the kitchen – "is she Mr Westcott's cook?"

Stanley grinned and shook his head. He grabbed a thick book lying open on the table and waved it in the air. In his haste, a book lying beneath it fell to the tiled floor with a thump. "Have you not heard of *Mrs Beeton's Book of Household Management*? My mother told me about it. The book's been a big help since Mr Westcott's cook left to take up a new position. I actually quite like cooking. I find recipes are a little like sums, as long you use the right proportions it mostly works out all right."

"Oh, I see," said Helena's father weakly. "Yes, I do believe my…wife owned a copy of that book."

Helena walked over and picked up the book which had fallen to the floor. *The Principles of Mathematics*. She frowned, placed it back on the table. What was this textbook doing in the kitchen? Her thought was pushed away by the sight of a plate of thin, black eels blanketed in white flour. She had never eaten eels before. Her mother had always bypassed them at the fishmonger's, favouring salted cod fillets instead. Helena swallowed, telling herself firmly it was good to try new things.

"I should probably explain," said Stanley. "I've found myself covering several jobs: butler, cook, gardener, and often housekeeper and, well, everything in addition to my role as a tutor." Stanley clamped his mouth shut as if he had perhaps said too much.

"But Father said Mr Westcott is very wealthy, so why

doesn't he employ servants?" asked Helena.

"Helena," whispered her father, his eyes narrowing.

"No, no. It's a good question," Stanley said, gesturing again for them to sit. He opened a cupboard and took out a wooden tray. On it he placed a starched-white linen cloth and a single gold-rimmed bowl. He poured some milk from a jug into a glass and placed it next to the bowl. "Things have been difficult here." He chewed on his bottom lip thoughtfully, as if trying to work out how much to tell them. "The staff have all left, you see. Miss Katherine Westcott employed me some months ago, and now I'm the only person left, so I'm trying to keep the house running the best I can, because if I don't, who will?"

Helena opened her mouth to ask the obvious questions. *Why have things been difficult? Why did Mr Westcott's servants leave? Mr Westcott has no children, so why does he need a tutor?*

But before the first letter of the first word could leave her lips, she saw her father was holding up a hand. It meant "stop at once", and she saw his eyes had the beginnings of a small fire behind them.

Helena closed her mouth and slumped back in her chair. She picked up a slice of apple and fed it to Orbit through the cage bars. It annoyed her greatly that her father thought asking questions in this house was not the done thing.

Stanley bustled around the kitchen, casting frequent glances at his cookery book as he coated the eels in egg and breadcrumbs and began to fry them on the range. While they sizzled and spat, he took the lid off a pot, ladled soup into two bowls and placed them in front of Helena and her father. Helena stared into the bowl. The soup was green and reminded her of an algae-filled pond.

Stanley frowned. "I hope the soup is all right. Mrs Beeton's recipe said to colour it with spinach juice, and I think I may have added a little too much."

"It is absolutely…delicious," said Helena's father firmly, taking a spoonful and swallowing. "Isn't it, Helena?"

Helena spooned the watery soup into her own mouth, the taste of spinach somewhat drowning out the asparagus. "Yes, it's lovely," she murmured.

Stanley prepared Mr Westcott's tray of food carefully, arranging a small bunch of rosy red grapes on a side plate. "You might think it a bit strange to see a man doing the cooking; my father certainly isn't too impressed I've taken on this role. But needs must, as they say," he said.

Helena wondered if perhaps Stanley was content to look after the eccentric Mr Westcott, and live in this bizarre house jammed to the rafters with clocks. But even if this was true, it really was quite bewildering to discover a grand household such as this having no cook or servants.

"I just need to take this upstairs," Stanley said, picking up the tray, his expression gloomier than before, as if talking about the changes in the house reminded him of things he preferred not to be reminded of.

There was a sudden scuffling noise in the hallway – like something had been dropped and was being retrieved. Stanley's eyes flickered towards the sound.

Helena saw him swallow, give a shake of his head (a movement so tiny she would have missed it if she had not been watching him). *Who was out there?* She glanced at her father, but he was busy scraping his bowl clean.

The tray in Stanley's hands wobbled as he hurriedly left the room.

Helena spooned another mouthful of soup to her lips. It was a little salty, but it was not the worst soup she had ever tasted (that award went to the meat broth dished up at school in winter). She sat back in her chair and wiped her lips on her napkin.

Her father looked up, smiled. "Aside from the unusual colour, this soup is rather good."

Another sound from the hallway. Urgent whispers.

Helena placed her napkin next to her bowl. "Actually, I don't think I'm very hungry. May I be excused?" she asked, straining to see round the door.

"Of course," her father said. "You do look a little pale. You must be weary after the journey. You go to bed. I will feed Orbit his apple and bring him up later."

Helena gave him a quick smile, pushed back her chair and darted from the room. She could hear Stanley's feet thumping up the stairs above her head. She was sure she could hear another lighter set of footsteps too. She was about to follow them when something caught her attention, in between an empty coat stand and a cupboard door. A piece of paper about as big as her palm was pinned to the wall. It was another pencil drawing of a flying machine. Even more detailed than the first, the wings and frame of the machine were ruler-straight, the rudder perfectly proportioned. She pulled it off the wall, traced a thumb over the tiny dent in the top of the paper left by a pin. Folding it in two, she slipped it into her pocket, listening to the two sets of footsteps carry on up the stairs to the floors above.

# CHAPTER 6

# Clock Room

Helena's father rapped on her bedroom door loudly. "I will see you on the ground floor in twenty minutes. We need to make a start on the clocks before breakfast." His voice was tinged with excitement.

Helena yawned and sat up in bed.

He knocked for a second time. "Did you hear me, Helena?"

"Yes, Father," Helena called, rubbing her eyes. It had been a disturbed night, what with the regular chiming of the clocks and the shouts and laughs from students enjoying their post-examination celebrations. She had imagined Cambridge to be a quiet and rather unassuming town and was beginning to realize she may have been mistaken. The clocks downstairs bonged and dinged and tinkled that it was seven o'clock. Reaching under her pillow, Helena pulled out and unfolded the drawing she had found pinned to the basement wall the night before. She traced a thumb over a wing of the flying machine and the rudder. Who had drawn it? Was it the same person who had left the mirror on Orbit's cage? Stanley had asked her to tell him about any more drawings found pinned to the walls, but she didn't want to, partly because of Katherine's instructions, but also because she wanted to discover who was drawing them and why.

Helena glanced at Orbit's cage, still covered with the night cloth. Climbing out of bed, she tentatively pulled it off, half expecting to see another piece of yellow ribbon – another gift. Orbit regarded her sleepily, but there were no new additions. Her bedroom door did not have a lock. Had she been foolish not to tell her father about the intruder to her room? He would not be pleased to learn someone had been meddling with their possessions. What if the intruder went into her father's room and broke some of his expensive clock tools?

She quickly pulled on a light-blue cotton day dress, her stockings and boots. She could not abide by Katherine's rule to not speak about something that could put her father's livelihood in danger.

Helena remembered the way Mr Westcott had looked at Orbit when they had arrived. It had been an odd combination of dislike and something else. Could *he* have attached the mirror? Could *he* be doing the drawings? But then again, she had not seen or heard him since they had left him in his study the previous afternoon. Even so, there was something eerie about his eyes that she couldn't put her finger on – like a slow-to-clear mist on a winter's morning. With a sickening lurch she remembered the contract her father had signed the day before. He had told her not to worry, but how could she not when all of their possessions would be lost if the clocks stopped?

By the time Helena had run downstairs to the ground floor, she was out of breath and agitated by her thoughts. The gold wedding-cake clock on the table in the hall emitted a fast *tick-tick-tick* in time with her heart that made her feel even more flustered. She stood and stared at it for a second or two. Small gold pots containing glinting jewelled flowers stood in the centre of each tier. It was an exotic and curious clock and looked very expensive.

She heard the creak of a floorboard, a low mutter from the room opposite Mr Westcott's study. *Father?* As she approached the door to the study, she slowed. Mr Westcott was inside speaking to someone in a low voice. He began to sound quite agitated. "It's your final warning, Marchington…no…I will not be commanded to listen. If you do not follow my precise instructions, you will be dismissed," she heard him say. It was a stilted one-sided conversation, which meant he must be using his telephone. Helena shrank away from the door, the floorboards groaning under her feet. Mr Westcott was clearly not someone to be crossed.

"Helena? Is that you?" her father called from the room opposite.

"Um…yes, Father, there is something I must talk to you…about," Helena said, forgetting about Mr Westcott and bursting into the room. She paused, something by the open door catching her eye. A chair. A boy sitting on the chair. He wore blue trousers, black shoes with brass hooks for the laces, and a white shirt with ruffles at the cuffs. His blond head of hair was turned towards her father.

Helena's father was standing on a stool examining a longcase clock with a pagoda-style top. "This mahogany clock is by Moore of Ipswich," he said. "Isn't it wonderful!" He placed a hand on it reverently.

Helena stared at Father. *Had he not seen the boy?*

The boy had swivelled in his chair to give Helena a sidelong glance. His blue eyes were narrowed and his lips set into a hard line.

"See the four dials at each corner of the clock face, Helena?"

Helena turned to her father.

"The clock shows us the day and month, allows us to select whether the mechanism should strike or be silent – and the fourth dial allows a choice of seven tunes. What a fine example this is," her father said, as proudly as if he'd made the object himself.

"I trust everything is to your satisfaction?" said a voice at the door. Mr Westcott. Helena turned. The chair the boy had been sitting on was empty. He had left the room without making a sound, like a ghost or a shadow. Helena remembered the sensation she had felt of being watched on the landing upstairs the night before. Her scalp tightened like a cap was being pulled onto her head.

Mr Westcott's eyes flickered to the empty chair then away again. He let out a long sigh. To Helena it sounded like butterflies' wings caught in a net, unhappy and striving to break free.

"Everything is…perfect, Sir," her father replied, stepping down from the stool and wiping his hands on his short apron. "This really is the most marvellous clock collection. Have you been collecting them for long?"

Mr Westcott walked slowly into the room. "No, not long," he said. His voice was fragile, light as a twig.

Between the ticks and tocks of the clocks, the silence in the room stretched until Helena thought it might snap.

"Well, you have made some excellent choices. I think they will increase in value over the coming years," said Helena's father.

"I am not interested in their value," Mr Westcott said, the crevices either side of his mouth deepening. "I merely need them to keep ticking."

Helena saw her father's Adam's apple bob in his throat as he swallowed. "Of course, Sir. And keep them ticking I shall." Her father threw Mr Westcott a broad smile. It was not returned.

"My sister – Katherine – likes to be present for the clock inspections," Mr Westcott said in a low voice, walking over to the clock Helena's father had just been looking at. "Every day," he added. His left eye twitched. He rubbed it. "I will leave you to your...work. It is Monday and I have a meeting with the board of directors at my printing firm."

"Of course, of course," Helena's father said.

Mr Westcott swivelled and left the room, giving the chair by the door one final glance.

"Who was that boy?" Helena asked as she passed her father the clock hood.

He replaced it with the same tenderness you might lay a baby in a cradle. "Excuse me?" he said.

"The boy...sitting by the door on that chair over there."

Her father turned and followed Helena's pointing finger to the empty chair. He pushed his hands into his jacket pockets. "I haven't the slightest idea what you are talking about."

Helena bit down hard on her bottom lip. How could her father not have seen him? It was as if this oppressive and strange house was causing her to see things which were not real.

"You do realize how important this position is for us, don't you, Helena?" her father asked softly.

Helena gave him a small nod.

He picked up a notebook and waved it at her. "I have been up half the night making a list of the clocks and the times we need to wind. We will be very busy, and that's aside from the conserving work I have to do. I will need your help."

"But...there's something I need to talk to you about..."

"Not now, Helena. I have work to do. Please can you check the pocket-watch cabinets upstairs, make a list of the sizes and types of watches and maybe sort out the winding keys?" He turned away, began to remove the hood of another clock.

Helena pressed her lips together, lowered her head and walked to the chair the boy had been sitting on. She laid a palm on the wooden seat. It was still warm. Which meant that the boy was not a ghost or a shadow at all, but someone else living in this house of one hundred clocks.

# CHAPTER 7

# The Girl

For the rest of that day, Helena followed her father around the house from room to room, carrying Orbit in his cage and writing out French verbs on the slate her school insisted she borrow so she wouldn't get behind. She assisted her father when he asked for help (*Pass me the small pocket-watch pliers, Helena. No, no, no, not those ones, the ones with the walnut handle. I need some pig's gut for the pendulum weights – measure it out, please*) and Helena's head swam with his instructions and orders, a constant reminder of the contract her father had signed. Ferocious bolts of anger would jolt her stomach like the strike of a match, her whole body burning at the thought of what their fate might be if they did not keep the clocks ticking. But Father was seemingly unconcerned, so fully absorbed in his work it was as if he had left their world entirely and entered another.

The mysterious boy would stealthily appear on the chair by the door of each clock room they entered, as if a magician had performed a clever trick. Helena tried catching his eye, but the boy always looked away.

When Helena and her father moved to the wisteria-wallpapered room of longcase clocks on the second floor, the boy followed, his footsteps as light as smoke. Helena remembered Katherine's instructions when they'd arrived, that they were not to speak about the things that they saw in the house, but her throat was itching with the urge to find out more about this boy. She knew that her father had seen him too, for his eyes had flitted to the boy and away again a few times throughout the day, but he had made no attempt to talk to him, Katherine's instructions clearly at the forefront of his own mind. While her father had been kneeling on the floor examining the bracketed feet of one of the clocks, Helena had kneeled beside him, asked quietly who he thought the boy was. Did he think he was perhaps Mr Westcott's son?

"Please don't ask such questions," Father had whispered with a ferocity that clenched Helena's jaw. *But how could she not speak of this?* Anyone feeling the eyes of another person on their back had a right to know who that person was and why they were staring so.

Helena tried broaching the subject of the boy and his parentage with Stanley after a lunch of anchovies on toast, and fresh lemonade so sour and lacking in sugar her tongue tingled. She asked him why Mr Westcott had failed to mention a boy lived in the house and if his presence was the reason Stanley had been employed as a tutor.

"Miss Westcott asked me not to speak about the happenings in this house," Stanley said glumly. He opened his mouth as if he wanted to expand on this statement, then closed it. He shook his head slightly, his dark hair ruffling.

Helena sat back in her chair. So Stanley had also been instructed not to speak about anything he saw in the house. Her curiosity expanded like hot metal.

Just before six o'clock that evening, the doorbell to

the house jangled. The boy had left the room half an hour before, his feet trudging up the stairs towards the top of the house. Helena and her father were still on the second floor in the room of longcase clocks, her father painstakingly removing the clock hoods, checking the brass dials, metal hands and weights. There came the sound of a distant door banging shut. Feet running down the stairs. Voices.

"*Ding-dong*-hickory-dickory-dock-clock-*tick-tock*," chattered Orbit.

The scent of sunshine, clear blue skies and rosy blooms swept into the room with Katherine, her long cream skirts whispering over the wooden floors like doves' wings. But she was not alone. A girl of about Helena's age was holding her gloved hand. Her leaf-green, chiffon dress caused a spark of envy to ignite inside Helena. The girl adjusted her hair clip with her free hand. Her blonde hair was short, emphasizing her petite nose and blue eyes.

Mr Westcott stood the other side of his sister, the skin under his eyes as dark as bruises, as he quickly glanced across at the girl, then away. His eyes were regretful, his lips trembling as if words were balancing on the tip of his tongue. The thought sprang into

Helena's head like one of Mr Westcott's fizzing electric lights. *Could this girl be his daughter? And if the girl was his daughter – surely the strange boy who sat in the clock rooms was indeed his son?*

"Have you been keeping up with your studies?" Katherine whispered to the girl, as she straightened the long white ostrich feathers on her own large and elaborate felt hat.

The girl looked up at Katherine solemnly. "Yes, Aunt Katherine," she whispered. The girl's eyes flicked to Mr Westcott, who sighed, straightened his shoulders a little and walked to the clock with the moon-faced pendulum bob. He laid his right palm on the clock door, his lips thinning as he watched the bob swinging back and forth. The cherubic moon-face swung in and out of view with a regularity that seemed to loosen some of the tightness in his shoulders.

"That is a very fine eight-day walnut clock by Vulliamy of London," her father said, walking over to the clock. "You are very lucky to have it in your collection. Vulliamy was clockmaker to the royal family in the eighteenth century."

"Yes, I am aware of that," said Mr Westcott coolly. He turned to face Helena's father. "You say I am lucky."

He said it as a statement, rather than a question, as if the word needed to be peeled back like orange skin to reveal something else altogether.

"Oh…your lovely parrot," said Katherine, letting go of the girl's hand and swishing over to the cage, which Helena had placed on her father's footstool.

"Hickory-dickory-dock. The mouse ran up the… *squawk, squawk, squawk,* hickory." Orbit jumped from his perch to the bottom of his cage and began to screech in alarm, his crown ruffling.

Helena froze. Why was he making that terrible noise?

Katherine clapped her hands together, a smile lighting up her face. "Oh, this bird is quite something. Don't you think so, Edgar?" she said above Orbit's cries.

*"Screech-screech-squawk."*

Helena saw the girl was chewing on her bottom lip, her eyes widening.

"Take him out of the room, Helena," her father said, rushing to the cage, his voice raised. "I am so sorry, Mr Westcott. He does not normally make such a fuss. It must be new people…new surroundings…"

Mr Westcott's cheeks were puce as he glared at Orbit bobbing about in his cage.

"*Squawk, squawk, squawk,*" cried Orbit, beating his wings against the metal bars.

"Shush, shush, pretty bird," said Helena, picking up the cage and walking swiftly to the door.

The girl's forehead furrowed in a sympathetic frown as Helena walked past her.

Helena's cheeks burned with embarrassment and her father threw her a disappointed glance as he turned back to Mr Westcott and the clocks. *Why had Orbit behaved so terribly, just when she had needed him to be on his best behaviour?*

At the door, Helena turned and looked back. Katherine was staring after her, a hand to her neck, fiddling with the buttons of her blouse. She gave Helena a quick and bright smile and turned away, the feathers on her hat wafting and waving, as if they had come alive and taken flight.

# CHAPTER 8

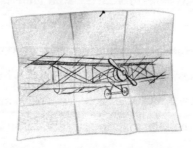

# The Message

Later that evening, long after dinner, Helena unpinned another drawing of a flying machine from the wall outside the longcase-clock room. Who was leaving them? She was certain now that the girl and boy were brother and sister and Mr Westcott's children. But which one of them was leaving the drawings and why? Katherine said Mr Westcott's wife had gone away eight months earlier. Gone away where? Were the boy and girl motherless too, like Helena? Except Helena wasn't quite motherless – not while she still had Orbit's voice to remind her of what she had lost.

Up on the third floor, Helena darted a quick glance back towards her room, where Orbit was now settled and sleeping. It was time to actively seek answers to some of her questions. She walked across the landing to the corridor of rooms where Stanley said Mr Westcott slept. The girl and boy must sleep up here too. There were two doors along each side of the corridor, and another at the very end. All of them were shut. It was so strange to think of Mr Westcott with all of his furniture and possessions here instead of downstairs. What had made him replace all of his things with clocks? Helena paused and tilted her head. The sound of voices drifted from behind the door at the end. Tiptoeing further along the corridor she suddenly stopped, scrunched up her toes in her stockings. It was one thing to overhear a conversation, but another to deliberately eavesdrop. But it was as if she couldn't stop herself. Perhaps if she didn't actually put her ear to the door, but instead smoothed the curled carpet runner with the toe of her stocking, she could linger long enough to hear something worth hearing.

"Very good, very good. Yes, that's exactly what I was saying." (Stanley)

"But would that adjustment keep it in the air for longer?" (It was the girl!)

71

"That's right, ask questions! It's the only way you can be sure you're learning the right things. Your aunt said those exact words to me herself." (Stanley)

"We have sent the letter, but will they read it?" (The girl)

There was a cough, the sound of feet moving over floorboards.

Helena quickly bowed her head and walked back down the corridor. It sounded like Stanley had been giving the girl a school lesson? But at this time of night?

After she had pulled on her nightdress and buttoned up the sleeves, Helena unfolded the most recent drawing she had found pinned to the wall downstairs. The girl had talked about "keeping it in the air for longer". Perhaps these *were* her drawings. If they were, she had a talent. Helena often wished she had a talent for something. She was quite hopeless at drawing, and the music lessons her mother had encouraged had been disastrous. The face of her music teacher, Miss Cartwright, contorted into pained expressions whenever Helena's fingers touched the piano keys.

But who were the drawings intended for? Was there a secret message hidden somewhere within the lines and angles? Maybe Stanley had helped her draw them.

Helena turned the picture over, traced a finger over the ridges the pencil had left in the paper. But there were no coded messages to be found. Helena heard the creak of bed springs in her father's room next door – he was so preoccupied he had gone to bed without coming to say goodnight.

With a sigh she re-folded the paper, pushed it under her pillow and was about to climb into bed herself when she heard the distant slam of the front door below her window, the sound of footsteps clicking on stone. It was late, a little after ten in the evening and ordinarily she would be asleep. Turning down the portable oil lamp (for she still distrusted the electric light on the wall), she pushed back the curtains and peered into the gloom. Mr Westcott...in a hat and coat was waiting at the kerbside. A hansom cab drew up, the horse snorting and bowing its head. The driver leaped down, and waited as Mr Westcott climbed in. The cab pulled away, the horse's hooves clattering down the street into the dark. Where was he going at this late hour?

"The last clockmaker has left the winding keys for the pocket watches in rather a muddle," Helena said to her father the following afternoon. She sat on the floor beside Orbit's cage, laying out the keys in front of her in order of size. Some were as small as a thumbnail – so tiny they could easily slip down between the floorboards. This thought had caused her to lay a green baize cloth over the boards – just in case. Imagine if they lost the only key to a watch and as a result it could not be wound! As much as she was angry at her father, and as much as she found working with clocks tiresome, she had to help make sure they returned home with all of their belongings.

"Once you have the keys in order, please can you wind the watches, Helena? This is our third day here and some have not been wound since the last clock winder left – they must be done today. I am going to the room next door to replace the pig's gut attached to some of the clock weights." He said this in a quick and distracted manner. Once again he had retreated into his "other" world of mechanical objects, somewhere she was not permitted or indeed welcome.

Helena sighed but nodded, glancing at the boy sitting on the chair by the door, as her father left the room with his box of tools. She chewed on the inside of her cheek. Was now the time to ask the boy about why he sat in the clock rooms day after day not saying a word?

Helena stood up and walked to the wooden pocket-watch cabinet and pulled open one of the drawers. The largest of the watches sat at the back of the drawer, the smaller ones at the front. Some were made of silver with fine engravings, some were gold with enamel-painted covers showing country scenes or delicate wild flowers. Helena picked up a gold watch emitting a fast tick-tick-tick-tick and carefully unscrewed the back. She selected a key which looked like it might fit, inserted it into the winding slot and gave it a few turns. Was that enough to keep the watch ticking? She didn't want to think about the consequences if it stopped. She replaced the back, gave it a quick polish and returned it to the cabinet. As much as she loathed to admit it, there was something rather hypnotic and lovely about these watches, their light and delicate ticks, the enamelled dials and engraved backs. *What stories could these watches tell if they could talk?* she thought. She wondered whose pockets they had lain in; what appointments they had helped people keep.

"I sometimes wonder that too," said a small voice.

*The girl!* Helena spun on her heels, her cheeks warm. She had been so absorbed in her task she had not realized that she had spoken out loud. Except…the girl wasn't there. But the boy was, just sitting looking at Helena as he chewed on his bottom lip. Helena frowned, took a step towards him. And another. There was something about him that was *different* from the boys she knew at school. She studied him harder. His small feet. His slim fingers resting in his lap. This…this wasn't a boy at all. It was a girl! A girl with a boy's haircut, wearing boys' clothes.

Helena blinked, thought about the girl she had seen the night before. She and this girl had the same eyes. The same nose. The same short hair. Could they be… yes they were! They were the same person. Helena felt the flush on her cheeks deepen. How peculiar. "Do you like clocks and watches?" she asked. The warmth on her cheeks heightened. It sounded so stupid. Of all the questions swilling around in her brain why had her lips chosen to pop that one out?

The girl's eyes clouded over and she looked at her knees. "Not especially," she said, in the same flat voice as before. "Not any more."

"Then why spend all of your time in the clock rooms?" asked Helena, her brow furrowing. She nibbled on a thumbnail. Her words sounded stupid – again! The questions Helena wanted to ask fluttered around in her head impatiently. Like, why did the girl dress in boys' clothes during the daytime? (Particularly when she clearly had lovely dresses she could wear instead.) Where was her mother? Why hadn't Mr Westcott mentioned that he had a daughter?

The girl pressed her lips together, did not reply. With a sigh she pushed herself up off the chair and walked out of the door, as if their brief conversation had never taken place.

Helena whooshed out a breath. "Well that didn't go very well." She bent to stroke Orbit's tail through the bars of his cage. Her cheeks felt tight and waxy as she noticed the small beginnings of a bald patch on Orbit's front where he had been gnawing at his feathers. This had never happened before. But then again Orbit had never been confined to his cage for such long periods of time before. Her mother had said pecking at feathers was a sign of boredom or frustration. She remembered his screeches last night during the clock inspection. Poor Orbit, his world had been thrown upside down as much as hers. At home he had been allowed to fly around in circles above her mother's head, squawking with delight. "You should have his tail feathers clipped," her father had once said. "One of these days he will fly through an open window and that will be the last we see of him."

Her mother had frowned and vehemently shaken her head. "Imagine if you were denied the right to be active. That is what it would be like for a bird who could not fly." And that was the end of it. Her father knew better than to argue with her mother over anything to do with her most beloved parrot.

Helena sighed, stood up and walked back to the pocket-watch cabinet. She picked up a large silver watch as big as her fist and unscrewed the back. Where was the hole for the winding key? She ran a finger over the smooth silver insides of the watch. How peculiar. She wasn't sure how to wind it. She gave the back a gentle tap, held it to her ear. It was ticking well, which meant the previous clockmaker had managed to wind it. She laid it face down in the drawer and ran her fingers around the rim. There was a gentle click and a hinge opened a second back, revealing a small compartment. Inside lay a small folded piece of card. Helena swallowed, looked back at the door. The girl had long gone. Her father's footsteps echoed from the floor above. Pulling the card out, she unfolded it. *Mr Fox. Watch & Clockmaker. Rose Crescent, Cambridge.* She turned the card over, her breath catching in her throat as she read the writing scrawled on the back.

*The clocks WILL stop for you too.*
*You WILL lose everything.*
*Leave, before it's too late!*

# CHAPTER 9

# Orbit's Escape

That night the ticks and tocks and chimes and strikes of the clocks on the floors below burrowed into Helena, each mechanical movement causing her to toss and turn in her bed. *The clocks WILL stop for you too.* That meant they had stopped already. For Mr Fox. Her stomach ached and she rubbed at the knot of tension that sat there, stubborn and unmoving. She knew she should tell Father about her worrying discovery, but at dinner that evening he had been quite distracted and pale, scribbling in his notebook while he spooned onion soup into his mouth. After he had scurried away to work on the clocks once more, Helena cleared the table while Stanley washed up. She saw his eyes flicker to several envelopes propped up on the windowsill. Stanley's eyes were hooded with tiredness as he scraped and scratched at onion burned onto the pot base. He sighed heavily. With a pang of remorse, Helena realized her own worries had caused her to lose sight of the fact that Stanley might have pressing concerns of his own.

Stanley turned, following Helena's gaze to the envelopes. "My mother writes weekly and gives me tips on how best to keep this household running, although she thinks it strange I see it necessary to do so. My father thinks I shouldn't be here at all, keeps asking when I'm returning to take up a position as an apprentice."

"Oh," said Helena.

"My father's an engineer, you see," continued Stanley. "*He* started as an apprentice in a workshop and now works for Mr Austin – a man who designs and builds automobiles. He thinks I should follow the same path as he did, not be here in Cambridge with all my books. Father is helping Mr Austin find premises for a new manufacturing plant…and when it's found he wants me to work in it."

"Goodness. Your father and Mr Austin think that the popularity of these automobiles will increase?" asked Helena, thinking about the rising number of vehicles she was now seeing on the roads in London. Her father thought they were marvellous inventions, often reminding Helena of how excited he'd been that the Locomotive Act of 1896 had seen the good sense to allow vehicles to increase their speed from two to fourteen miles per hour in town. But to Helena these machines were noisy and cumbersome (and were often seen broken down at the side of the road). She preferred the sound of horses' hooves on cobbles to the vibrations of wheels and screech of brakes.

"Yes, the automobile's popularity is growing daily," said Stanley. "Mr Austin says there are around twenty thousand on the country's roads now and there could be four times that in the next five years. But I don't want to work as an apprentice. There's so much more I'd like to know about engineering, things I can't learn in a workshop. I had a teacher at school who persuaded my parents I should try for a scholarship to the boys' high school. It turns out I'm rather good at learning, much to my parents' surprise, and now, here I am."

"And so now you work here as a tutor?" asked

Helena, hoping he would tell her a little more about the girl and the lessons he was giving her.

Stanley nodded. "I saw Miss Westcott's advertisement in *The Times* newspaper for a tutor. At the interview I saw Mr Westcott's collection of academic books, which I thought might assist me with my own education and allow me to save some money too. I accepted the position gladly, but things have turned out a little differently to what I imagined."

"Oh, I see," said Helena, as she wiped crumbs from the table. That explained the mathematics book in the kitchen. Stanley was tutoring the girl while also undertaking his own studies. But in addition to that, he was trying to run an entire household on his own. It all seemed rather unfair.

Accepting that sleep was not going to come that night, Helena slipped out of bed and pulled on her woollen socks and a cardigan. Orbit snickered under his night cloth. She lifted it and he peeked at her.

"Mother loves Helena, Mother loves Helena." Orbit's voice was as gentle as falling snow. "Lovely bird, lovely bird, you're a lovely, lovely, bird," he said, bobbing his head and laughing. It was her mother's laugh. Bright and tinkling and like a spring waterfall.

*A flash of memory – a day trip to go strawberry picking. Her mother's lips stained red and laughing as the sun beat down on their backs.*

Helena's tongue suddenly felt swollen and too big for her mouth. "Laugh again. Please, Orbit. Laugh again." Helena held onto the bars of the cage and closed her eyes, imagined Mother was kneeling beside her in her cream lace dress, smelling of lavender and hope. She lowered her head and brushed a tear from her cheek. "Laugh again, Orbit. Please, lovely bird." But now, distracted by the mirror, Orbit was tapping at it repeatedly, filling the room with tinny pings. Helena never quite knew when Orbit would mimic Mother's laugh. He could go weeks singing the nursery rhymes Mother had taught him and chattering absolute nonsense, and then clear as day her mother's tinkling laugh would send ghostly shivers of remembering down her spine. Father used to watch Helena tight-lipped, in the days and weeks after Mother's death, as she sat in front of Orbit's cage waiting for him to imitate the one person she wished she could still talk to. When Mother had gone it was like a whirlpool had sucked all of the happiness from the house and Orbit was the only thing that could even a quarter of the way return it.

Helena heard her father cough next door, the squeak of his bed springs. It would not do to disturb him, but that would certainly happen if she did not stop Orbit from playing with the mirror. Unlocking the cage, she opened the tiny door and scooped him out, cupping him in her hands. Placing him inside her cardigan, she buttoned it up until just his head was peeking out. Mother would do this sometimes when he was unsettled and it would calm him, claiming the sound of her heart beating like a drum would be soothing. She would take him for a short walk along the corridor until he settled.

Creeping from her room, Helena ignored the shadows and dark corners, let Orbit nibble on a finger (which nipped but at least kept him quiet). At the top of the stairs she stood and listened, the steady thrum of the clocks drifting upwards. A stifled cough on the floor below. She peered over the bannister, heard the creak of a door. She glanced down the corridor to her father's room. All was silent now. The other corridor was quiet too. Taking a deep breath, she tiptoed down the stairs, pausing on the bottom step. A light…coming from the longcase-clock room. Helena crept to the door.

The sound of breathing came from inside, fast and furious. "My darling Evangeline. My boy," a voice said.

Helena shrank back into the shadows. *Mr Westcott's voice.*

"Will it happen again? My clocks...I fear I am sinking under the pressure to keep them ticking."

Orbit wriggled, let out a small snicker at the same time the clocks chimed, marking half past the hour. Helena's feet froze to the floorboards. Had the clocks disguised the fact she was sneaking around Mr Westcott's house at night, overhearing things she most definitely should not be overhearing?

"My clocks...my clocks...always ticking. It cannot be otherwise...for that would be opening the door to all manner of terrible things..." Mr Westcott murmured.

A pull on the sleeve of her cardigan. Helena started in shock, her mouth opening to form a cry. It was the girl, standing before her in a long white cotton nightdress – her eyes wild and wide as a stormy sky, her short hair standing up in tufty peaks. She pulled on Helena's sleeve again, pressed a finger to her lips, then pointed to a closed door two along from where they were standing.

Orbit snickered again.

As Helena and the girl stood listening, the ticks and

tocks seemed to quieten. The girl's lips thinned and she grabbed Helena's hand and pulled her down the corridor.

Helena and the girl stood in silence in the skeleton-clock room, the brass mechanisms beneath their glass domes glinting in the moonlight spilling between a gap in the heavy blue and cream curtains.

Helena held Orbit close to her chest, ignored his increasingly painful nips on her finger.

The girl pressed her right ear to the door, a lock of hair falling over her cheek. "He's gone now," she said softly, her voice crackly, like it needed moistening with some of Helena's father's clock oil.

"Mr Westcott…is he your father?" Helena whispered.

The girl nodded solemnly.

"I'm Helena," Helena whispered, thinking that she might have gathered this already from overhearing conversations between her and her father in the clock rooms.

"I'm Boy," whispered the girl, fiddling with a button on the cuff of her nightdress.

*That was the name she had overhead Mr Westcott say in*

*the clock room.* "But...that isn't a name," said Helena, wrinkling her nose. Standing there barefoot in her long nightdress she very much looked like a girl and Helena wondered how she could ever have thought otherwise.

"Well it's *my* name," Boy whispered fiercely. Her eyes softened as she looked at Orbit, who was wriggling and squirming inside Helena's cardigan. Her parrot had been well behaved, but as Helena had learned in the past, you should never expect too much from a Blue-fronted Amazon.

"Ouch," Helena whispered, as Orbit craned his neck and pecked at her arm. "Oh, please, Orbit...be good. I'll take you upstairs to your cage in a minute." But those were not the words Orbit wished to hear. With one almighty wriggle, he popped off one of the buttons on Helena's cardigan which bounced and rolled along the floorboards and with a giant swoosh of his wings, flapped up to the ceiling, grazing the dome of a very tall, and expensive-looking, brass skeleton clock. Helena stared in dismay at her precious bird, her pulse thudding in her ears. If Orbit damaged any of the clocks in here, she and her father would be sent packing...but not before Mr Westcott had taken all of their things away.

# CHAPTER 10

# Boy

"No," whispered Helena. "Oh gosh…Orbit. Come down at once."

But Orbit ignored Helena. Why would he choose to obey her when he could at long last stretch out his wings, feel the rush of air between his feathers? Orbit swooped, his wings catching against another glass clock dome, which rattled and shook.

"Careful," whispered Helena.

Orbit was flying in dizzying circles, small squawks of satisfaction echoing around the room.

"Orbit. Please come down. We'll get in the most

tremendous trouble," Helena ordered in her sternest whisper.

Boy was standing with her back to the door, her eyes wide with delight, her head tilted to the spectacle above as if she were watching the greatest circus performance she had ever seen.

There was a loud thump and the scrabbling of claws.

Horror climbed Helena's spine like a vine. Orbit had landed on one of the shelves built into the walls of the room. The wood had been polished to a high shine and his claws clicked as he walked along its length, occasionally bending his neck to peck at the clocks resting on the shelf.

"Oh no," Helena said in a strangled gasp. "Boy – please help me! If Orbit damages the clocks…"

In a flash Boy was standing in front of the shelf, thrusting out her right arm as if she expected Orbit might choose to fly down and land on it.

Orbit gave Boy an imperious stare and continued tapping at the glass dome of a clock with his beak.

"He won't come down on his own. We need something to stand on, so we can catch him," whispered Helena, sure that at any moment the dome would shatter, littering the floor with a million ice-like pieces of glass.

Boy turned and ran to the door. For an anxious second Helena thought she was going to fetch her father to come and help. But instead she picked up the wooden chair beside the door and carried it to the shelf. Helena took a step towards it, but Boy had already leaped onto it.

"Orbit doesn't know you. Be careful, he does sometimes nip strangers…" Helena paused. Orbit had stopped pecking at the glass dome. He sidled along the shelf, his feet clicking and tapping until he and Boy were at eye level.

Orbit bobbed his head. "Hello, hello, hello. Jack and Jill ran up the hill," he said in a throaty gurgle.

Boy held out her hand. Helena saw it was trembling. Orbit hopped onto Boy's wrist and walked up her arm, giving her nightdress an exploratory nip. Boy lowered herself on the chair until she was crouching, and Helena slowly reached across and gathered Orbit to her. He didn't resist, just pecked affectionately at her fingers.

Helena sank to the floor and cupped Orbit in both hands, the thrum of his small heart pulsing into her palms. "Thank you," she said, relief bustling through her.

A rosy flush crept up Boy's neck. She gave Helena a small smile, the type one conspirator gives another to let them know their secret is safe.

"Why is your bird called Orbit?" Boy's voice was reed-thin. She licked her lips, waited.

Helena could hear Boy's breaths, short and fast and expectant. "It was my mother who named him," she said quietly. Boy looked at her, waited for her to continue. "She said…that when he flew, he orbited her, like the Earth orbits the Sun."

Boy tilted her head and smiled, as if this explanation pleased her.

Orbit wriggled in Helena's hands as words rose inside her, like bubbles. "Why is your name Boy? And why do you dress like one? Is it you who draws pictures of flying machines and pins them to the walls…and gave Orbit that present? And…why is your father so… obsessed with clocks?" Helena paused, sucked in a shaky breath. She knew she had bombarded Boy with too many questions.

"My mother had a bird once," Boy said, reaching to stroke Orbit's crown. "He was called Maximilian. I thought Orbit might like the mirror he used to play with. It's sad my father says he must stay locked in his cage all day."

"Where is your mother now?" Helena asked

cautiously. She didn't want to scare Boy off, have her clam up like last time, but equally she needed some answers to the puzzles this house had presented.

"She's in France," Boy said softly. "She has been since last October."

"Do you mean…on holiday?" Helena asked, thinking that was a rather long time for her to be apart from her family.

Boy's eyes began to cloud over.

"Sorry," Helena said. "I'm asking too many questions, aren't I? If Father were here, I would get a rather large telling off for being impolite."

Boy stared at Helena for a second, as if thinking about what Helena had just said.

"I think it's jolly sad your mother is not around. You must miss her," said Helena.

"I do, very much," said Boy. Her hand smoothed down Orbit's tail feathers. "Where is your mother?"

"Oh…she…um…she…died," said Helena.

Boy's eyes widened.

"It's all right…really. It was almost a year ago and I am just about growing used to it."

Boy threw Helena a disbelieving look and pressed her lips together.

Helena sighed. "Well actually, it's not all right at all. I miss her…every day. Sometimes it's hard to think of anything else." Helena swallowed. "But I have Orbit to remind me of her. And I still have Father, even though he spends more time in his clock workshop than at home."

"Our fathers are similar then," said Boy glumly.

"Mmm. Maybe," said Helena, thinking that actually their fathers were quite different, and she would not want to exchange Boy's icicle-eyed father for her own in a million or more years.

"My father spends most of his time at his printing firm. And when he's at home he's…distracted by the clocks," said Boy, pulling her knees up inside her nightdress and looping her arms around them.

Helena thought of her own father's lengthy evenings at work back in London, sometimes returning long after she had settled Orbit and gone to bed. Perhaps their fathers *were* more similar than she had thought.

Boy suddenly sprang to her feet and flung out her arms, whirled around on the spot. "This skeleton-clock room used to be the library. We would all play board games in the evenings in front of the roaring fire. Father and Mother would laugh then."

"Will you be in the clock rooms tomorrow?" asked Helena, thinking that Boy was rather intriguing, and she would like to get to know her better.

Boy nodded. "Will you?" she asked, giving Helena a shy smile.

"Yes," replied Helena, giving a warm smile in return. "Well, I suppose I had better get Orbit back to his cage before he causes any further trouble." As they left the room, Helena stared at the yawning fireplace, the bare walls and floors, the relentlessly ticking clocks. It was hard to imagine this had once been a room filled with laughter and happiness. She was certain something rather terrible had happened to Mr Westcott and his family to make things the way they were now.

# CHAPTER 11

# Clock Parts

Helena glanced again at the chair by the door of the pocket-watch room. Boy had not come to any of the clock rooms that morning. She had said a quiet goodnight to Helena at the top of the stairs the night before and padded back to her room, Helena making a mental note of the door she disappeared behind. What a peculiar name Boy had. It was strange that her mother was in France. Did his wife's absence explain why Mr Westcott seemed so sad and unbalanced, like he was a pair of scales and too many weights had been placed on one side of his brain? Boy had the same small, sad sapphire-blue eyes as her father. But Helena thought that perhaps they hadn't always been that way. She could imagine the skin at the edges creasing with laughter quite frequently. Perhaps she could help make Boy smile. It would be nice to have a friend to talk to in this strange house.

"Helena...come quickly," said her father rather breathlessly from across the room, his clock pliers dropping from his hand to the floor with a thud.

Helena pushed all thoughts of Boy away and turned in a dizzying rush to see her father standing hunched over a table. *Perhaps he had found another message from Mr Fox.*

"Look at this most marvellous marine chronometer," he said, beckoning her forward.

"A chronometer," Helena repeated, her heart slowing to a steadier beat.

"It was hidden in the bottom of the cabinet, an original, made by John Harrison himself. I knew this particular one had been auctioned off by Harrison's family, but to see it here...in this house...well," her father said, his eyes hazy.

Helena crinkled her nose. Her father's voice was charged with emotion. She looked at the object that had captured his attention. Resting in a plain wooden box, it looked like a silver pocket watch that could have belonged to a giant. It was certainly unremarkable compared to some of Mr Westcott's other fancy clocks. "It's…nice," said Helena with a shrug.

"Nice?" Her father's voice was incredulous. "Don't you remember me telling you how Harrison solved the mystery of discovering a ship's longitude at sea – its position to the east or west?"

Helena shook her head. Her father had told her many stories about clocks and watches over the years and they all tended to fade, like rain falling on cobbles on a hot day.

"Thousands of sailors perished before the invention of this device," her father continued excitedly. "Ships would be dashed to pieces on the rocks or be raided by pirates because they could not chart their position accurately." He pulled on a pair of cotton gloves and held the clock as if it were fragile and liable to disintegrate in his hands at any moment. "Listen," he said, holding it to Helena's ear. "What do you hear?"

*Tick-tick-tick-tick-tick-tick-tick-tick-tick-tick.*

"It's got a fast mechanism," Helena said, looking at the clock in surprise. "Faster than the other clocks."

"Yes. Five ticks per second, to be precise," said her father with a smile. "That is what makes it able to keep accurate time at sea. The mechanism inside this chronometer changed the world. And made John Harrison a wealthy man – he claimed much of the large prize offered by Parliament in 1714 for the first person to solve the longitude problem. Not without a little fuss mind you, but that is a story for another time."

*How surprising*, thought Helena, making a mental note to perhaps listen a little more carefully to Father's stories in the future. It was rather interesting how a clock could change the world so. She glanced at the cabinet of pocket watches and thought again about Mr Fox's hidden message. It seemed a few of the clocks in this house had interesting stories to tell.

Her father placed the chronometer back in the cabinet and opened a long drawer. He picked up one of the pocket watches lying inside. "Can you reach in and reattach the spring in this watch?" asked her father. "Your fingers are smaller than mine."

Helena bent over the cogs and wheels. Squinting, she reached inside and slowly refixed the chain.

Her father examined it closely, gave her a nod of approval. "Well done. You are picking things up quickly. It pleases me that you are showing an interest, Helena."

Despite Helena's still-rumbling anger at her father, a small glow of satisfaction rolled through her.

"I need to go out for a short while. I must pick up some mechanical parts and pig's gut from a shop on Regent Street," her father said, closing the back of the watch.

"I could go," said Helena eagerly.

"Hmm, I am uncertain as to whether going into Cambridge on your own is a good idea," her father replied.

"Please, Father. I will be back before you know it and I do so want to see the town."

Helena's father stroked his beard, glanced at the window and the weak sun struggling to break through the low cloud.

"We have been here for three days, and it would be nice to take some fresh air. I could complete some of the observation work Miss Jacobs asked me to do while I am away from school." Helena very much hoped this would do the trick. Father was always so particular about her keeping up with her studies, even though much of the time Helena did not quite see how the lessons would provide her with the skills she required to be a grown-up. Lessons in observation took place at the end of each school day and consisted of writing down the things they could see outside the school window. It was dull work and the observations did not vary much unless there was a change in the weather.

Her father looked a little more convinced. "Well, perhaps Stanley can give you directions…"

"Yes! I shall go and ask him at once," said Helena, picking up Orbit's cage.

Her father smiled wearily, and Helena noticed with dismay the dark smudges under his eyes. "Thank you. It will give me more time to work on these watches," he said.

Helena returned his smile, swallowing the small burn of guilt. For as much as she enjoyed her father's praise, she had only one thing on her mind that morning – the message on Mr Fox's card. An opportunity had presented itself and she needed to pay his Rose Crescent shop a visit to understand exactly what the message hidden in the pocket watch meant.

# CHAPTER 12

# Cambridge

Helena dragged in a deep breath of air as she walked along Trumpington Street towards Mr Fox's shop on Rose Crescent. The card she had discovered hidden inside the watch, with its strange message, felt like a hot stone in her skirt pocket. The drawstring cloth bag she carried on her shoulder jiggled. "Shush, Orbit," she murmured. Mother had made the bag especially for her parrot, lining it with soft midnight-blue velvet and making regular cuts in the fabric for ventilation (and so Orbit could stick out his head and watch the world go by – something he loved to do on the streets of London). He had become a familiar sight at their local parade of shops, people stopping to enquire after his health and encouraging him to talk and sing. Since reading Mr Fox's warning message, Helena had decided she could not leave Orbit alone in Mr Westcott's house – even if Father had promised to supervise him. Perhaps the fresh air would be a welcome change for her parrot, stop him from chewing on his feathers, which had been landing on the bottom of his cage with alarming regularity over the past day.

"Hickory-dickory," Orbit squawked. Two men on bicycles in candy-cane-striped jackets looked and laughed, tipped their straw boater hats to Helena and cycled on.

The hems of Helena's skirts dipped into the fast-flowing water of an open drain as she crossed the street. The day was dull, drifts of mist obscuring the sun and bringing a chill to the air. But despite this, Helena's shoulders straightened with relief at being outdoors, after being stuck inside Mr Westcott's oppressive house.

She glanced at Stanley's hastily drawn map. She needed to continue down the street past Peterhouse

College and King's College Chapel until she reached the market square. When Helena had asked how she would know when that would be, Stanley had simply said, "King's College Chapel needs no description, Helena. You'll know it when you see it."

"I say, did you know that my rooms at Christ's College are next to old Charles Darwin's?" said a young man leaning against the Peterhouse College railings (who sounded like he'd swallowed a plum). "Saw some of his beetle collections – rather extraordinary it was."

"I heard his son, George, giving an astronomical lecture last term – fascinating chap," replied his friend, as Helena walked past. Astronomy. Botany. There was so much to know in the world – and it seemed here was the place to learn it. A grand stone-pillared archway guarded the entrance to Peterhouse, and she paused to peer through to a small chapel and a courtyard beyond. The place had a hushed air of tranquillity and privacy about it. It was so different from the London suburbs, where children played out on the street with skipping ropes, and mothers chatted over garden fences while pegging out the washing.

Helena eagerly drank in her surroundings as she walked, the smart tailor's shop displaying the black gowns and mortar-board caps she had seen students wearing as they hurried between buildings. She watched a horse-drawn tram rumble past, the boards around the top deck advertising soap and coal and carriages for hire for weddings and funerals. A man on the top deck of the carriage stood up and pointed down the street. He was wearing a smart hat. Helena followed his gaze. He could only be pointing at one thing – the enormous buff-coloured, stone building with stained-glass windows. Helena hurried onwards, until she reached a small parade of shops. She stopped under one of the awnings and stared up at King's College Chapel. London had some magnificent structures – St Paul's Cathedral, the Houses of Parliament – but this was a different kind of building altogether. The spires, turrets and glinting windows reaching into the mist made her feel a little dizzy and ant-like. A group of chatting young women carrying bundles of books bumped into her back, nudging her from her daydream.

Orbit squawked. "All fall down. All fall down."

"Oh, a parrot," said a tall woman with wayward hair and very straight teeth. "How glorious."

"Come on, Esther. We need to return these books to the library," one of the other women said.

Esther gave Helena a quick wave and ran after her friend.

Helena stared after them, remembering the article from the newspaper Mother had read aloud last year. While women could study at Cambridge University and learn about things like natural science and geology, just as Charles Darwin had, they were still not allowed to gain a degree at the end of their studies. *How terrible*, Helena had thought glumly, while she sucked on a pear drop and played with Orbit.

"It is such a pity that men and women cannot be equals," her mother had said. "Helena is bright and intelligent and interested in all things. Look at how the world is changing, Isaac. We have electricity and automobiles and people are taking to the skies in these tremendous flying machines. Why should she be denied the same choices as men when deciding what to make of her life?"

"I agree with you, my dear," her father had answered. "But, sadly, not all people are as forward-thinking as the Clockmakers' Company. It was only ten years after the Great Fire of London that *they* took on their first female apprentice."

Helena's mother had smiled, glanced at Helena, who

was stacking wooden blocks on the floor for Orbit to knock over. "Helena will have more opportunities in her lifetime. I am sure of it."

Helena knew she wanted more. She felt it deep in her bones and in her whole being. But more of *what* was the question. She had so many questions that required answers. She certainly did not want to spend the rest of her life wearing pretty dresses and sitting in a dimly lit parlour darning or knitting or painting or doing observational studies – all the things she was hopeless at. But while she did not know what she wanted to do when she was grown up, she felt the sting of this inequality keenly. She knew she could do the same as any boy, and one day she would.

She turned away from the students and pulled out her pocket watch. She needed to hurry; she must not keep Father waiting. She would visit Mr Fox, find out exactly why he had placed that message in a pocket watch of Mr Westcott's, then collect the clock parts. She was acutely aware that she could not be the cause of the clocks stopping and them losing all of their things. An image sprang into her head of Orbit's cage swinging in Mr Westcott's hand, the portrait of her family jammed under his other arm, as he strode off into the setting sun with all of their worldly goods.

With a quick glance at the map, she jammed her hands into her pockets and headed towards Fox's clockmaker's shop, her heart thudding uncomfortably in her chest.

# CHAPTER 13

# Mr Fox's Shop

Fox's Watch & Clockmaker's shop was built into the curve of Rose Crescent, a half-moon shaped and almost hidden street, which joined the bustling market square. Helena swallowed the onion-sized lump that sprang into her throat as she looked in the shop window. The shop looked deserted. There was no gleaming display of watches and clocks, just a long maroon cloth bearing the imprints of objects that were no longer there.

Since Helena's mother had died, one of her father's favourite weekend pastimes was finding new clock shops to visit in London, where he would spend an age examining the contents of the radiant window displays, while Helena fidgeted and yawned.

*What had happened to all of Mr Fox's clocks and watches?*

Helena pushed open the shop door and the bell jangled.

Orbit shifted in his bag and his beady eyes blinked. "Three blind mice, three blind mice, *snicker*."

"How curious, Orbit," Helena whispered, stroking his head. The glass display cabinets inside the shop were also empty. The wooden countertop was bare. The door behind the counter was shut. Perhaps she should knock, see if Mr Fox was out the back? Glancing at the shop door, she noticed something she had not seen when she came in. The door sign looking back at her said "Open". Which meant the sign on the outside of the door must have said "Closed". Helena felt a sudden heaviness in her legs. *Fox's Watch & Clockmaker's was no longer in business.*

Making a quick decision, she dipped underneath the counter and rapped lightly on the door behind it. A creaking noise above her head – someone was on the floor above. She knocked again, harder this time.

A cough. Not a man's cough, though, more like a child's.

Opening the door, she peered up the dark stairs. "Hello. I am looking for Mr Fox. Is he about?" No reply. Another creak of the floorboards. Someone was definitely up there. Why were they not coming down? "Hello," she called again. "I've come from Mr Westcott's house. I would very much like…to speak to Mr Fox."

*Creak-creak-creak-creak.*

Footsteps hurtling down the stairs towards her. A boy of no more than ten stood before her, a wiry figure with a shock of dark hair, clenched fists and nostrils flared as a pony's. "Go away. We don't have anything else for you to take," he said, his voice wavering.

The bag on Helena's shoulders wobbled and Orbit snickered quietly.

Helena stared at him. "I…just want to speak to Mr Fox."

"You said you've come from Mr Westcott's," the boy said, his wide eyes fixed on Orbit's bag, which was rocking and swaying.

Helena nodded. "Yes…that's where my father is employed. Like I said…"

"Your father. Is he a clock winder and conservator for

111

Mr Westcott, like my pa was?" the boy asked, taking a step closer. Helena caught a whiff of unwashed clothes and skin and swallowed the urge to pinch her nose.

"Um…yes. He started work there a few days ago. We're from London and…"

Without warning the boy grabbed her hand, turned and began to pull her up the stairs.

"Hey," Helena said sharply. "Let go of me this instant." She twisted her arm, trying to loosen his hold, but the boy's grip was too firm and he yanked her up two more of the steps.

"*Squawk, squawk, squawk,*" yelled Orbit in alarm.

Helena clawed at the wall with her free hand to stop herself from spiralling down the stairs and landing in a very inelegant heap at the bottom, injuring herself and Orbit. But the boy kept on pulling her forward until they reached the top of the stairs.

It was there that Helena finally shook herself free and quickly checked on Orbit. His feathers were ruffled and his bead-like eyes regarded her with indignation. Helena knew how he felt. She plonked her hands on her hips and glared at the boy. "What do you think you're doing? You can't just go around grabbing a girl's hand and…oh…" Her words caught in her mouth. To the left of the stairs was a small room. On the floorboards, under a large Georgian window were huddled two small, hollow-cheeked girls, both with the same straight black hair as the boy. One girl was sucking her thumb, the other sat with her back to the wall, her knees hugged to her chest.

"My sisters," the boy said limply. Helena glanced at him. His eyes were watery. It was as if the fight and strength he had shown her downstairs had suddenly been sucked away. "I'm Ralph," he said in a low voice. "Ralph Fox." He fiddled with his shirt collar. It was missing a button.

Helena looked from him to his sisters and back again, a terrible thought worming its way into her gut. "Your father is Mr Fox?" she said hesitantly.

Ralph nodded.

"He…worked for Mr Westcott?"

Ralph nodded again.

One of the girls began to cry quietly. "Mama!" she said through her tears. "When is she coming back?"

Ralph walked over to her, kneeled down and wiped her face with his shirtsleeve. "When she's got some food and found us somewhere to live," Ralph said softly. "Don't worry, Hettie. She won't be long."

Helena's heart kicked hard in her chest. The room was empty – there was nothing except a metal pail of water in the corner and two tin cups. "Is this your home?" she asked.

"Used to be," said Ralph, his voice loaded with misery. "Until we lost all of our things."

"Lost them?" Helena said, thinking of the contract she was not supposed to mention.

"Well…not lost. Mr Westcott took them. The clocks stopped and he took everything from us. All the furniture, our pictures – even the ugly one of our dead aunt who nobody liked. He took all of Pa's clocks and tools too. Everything is gone, including young Mr Phillips who worked as Pa's assistant in the shop. Pa can't even make a living now. He borrowed money to rent this shop. And for his equipment. He borrowed and borrowed and it was going to be all right, because Mr Westcott was going to pay him a small fortune for keeping the clocks ticking and Pa could have paid off his debts. But now it's all gone wrong and we have nothing."

"But…but…when did this happen?" asked Helena, fear gripping its icy fingers around her heart.

Ralph's shoulders sagged. "A few weeks back. You said your pa is working for Mr Westcott now?"

Helena nodded.

"Did Mr Westcott make him sign any papers? Pa is spending all his days at Mr Westcott's solicitor's office, trying to get these papers terminated, I think the word was."

Helena brought her hands to her flaming cheeks. *Mr Westcott had made Ralph's father sign a contract too. And the clocks had stopped and now they had nothing.* She clutched Orbit's bag a little tighter and thought of her father waiting for the clock parts she was to collect, which would allow him to disappear back into his world of mending and maintenance.

Ralph's face twisted in anger. "You need to leave that house of clocks. Right now. Don't wait for the clocks to stop, for they will. My pa looked after them proper well. He is…was…the best clockmaker in Cambridge and everyone knows it. He was so good, Ma never needed to work. She says she regrets that now."

"Clocks-clocks-clocks," snickered Orbit.

Helena looked at Ralph in horror. She pulled the small card from her coat pocket, held it out to him. "I found this…hidden in a watch."

Ralph took it from her. "Pa's writing," he said, with a sniff. "It was a warning. But looks like it came too late.

The clocks will stop for you too. Mr Westcott will take all of your things and you will end up in the workhouse on Mill Road – just like we probably will."

# CHAPTER 14

# Pebbles

The chill of the eddying mist. The shouts and cries of market sellers. The chatter of university students. The ring of bicycle bells. Orbit's gentle snickers and squawks and nibbles on her coat sleeve. Helena noticed none of these things as she left Ralph and his sisters. Her head pulsed in time with her footsteps as she walked. Her father was as good a clockmaker and winder as Mr Fox, she was sure of it. But the clocks had stopped for Mr Fox despite his best efforts. Whatever had Mr Westcott done with the Fox family's possessions? How could he have left them with nothing? Those hungry little girls sitting on the floorboards. Ralph was right – they would end up in the workhouse if their father and mother had no means of providing food or making a living. If Mr Fox had been in debt, the well-paid clock conservator position at Mr Westcott's house must have seemed like the answer to all of his problems. But his plan to make money had backfired in the most dreadful way.

Helena and her father occasionally walked past the workhouse close to where they lived in London. Her eyes would be drawn to the red-brick building, which reminded her of newspaper pictures she had seen of industrial mills in the north, tall and forbidding. Helena knew that to end up in a workhouse was something to be avoided at all costs. It was a last resort for the poor and homeless, even though it provided them with a roof to sleep under, regular meals and clothes. But in return people were expected to work long, tedious hours. They would hear the sounds of men in the yard, chopping wood, crushing stone – hard physical labour that would earn them just enough money to stay there. Tendrils of steam would rise from the open windows as women washed and scrubbed in the laundry. "Those people in there have fallen on hard times indeed," her father would say sadly. "There must be nothing worse for a person's self-esteem and health than ending up in the workhouse."

Helena's heart began to sink into her boots as she finally walked up the steps to Mr Westcott's town house. The building loomed above her like a grumpy giant, its many windows glaring at her as a sudden burst of raindrops hit the ground. Her hand was reaching up for the brass door knocker, when a flash of pain hit the back of her right calf. "Ouch," she said, bending to rub her leg. What had just happened? She swivelled, saw a boy of about her age standing by a box hedge near the bottom of the steps, then glanced down at a medium-sized pebble lying beside her right boot.

"Did you throw that at me?" Helena asked incredulously, bending to pick it up. The pebble was warm in her hand, as if it had been held in someone's fist for a while.

The boy was standing rod straight, but Helena thought she saw his chin wobble. His shoes were polished to a high shine and his shirt collar was starched and white as a snowdrop. He didn't dress like the type of street boy who hurled pebbles at strangers.

Helena took a step forward. "I said, did you throw that pebble?"

Orbit popped his head out of the cloth bag at the exact same moment the boy whipped another pebble from his pocket and hurled it in Helena's direction. She ducked, and instead of hitting her or the parrot, the pebble hit Mr Westcott's grey front door with a dull thud.

Helena's skin bristled with indignation as the patter of rain intensified.

The boy took another pebble from his pocket and hurled it over Helena's head. It bounced off the door and down the steps, narrowly missing Orbit.

"Listen here. You stop that right now…" shouted Helena, running down the steps towards the boy.

"*Squawk, squawk, squawk,*" cawed Orbit. "Pop goes the weasel, Mother, Mother, *squawk!*"

"Miss Graham!"

Helena froze. The boy's face paled and he turned and began to sprint down the street.

Helena turned. Mr Westcott's hands were clenched into fists by his sides, his face even greyer than usual.

She felt a burst of hot indignation at the terrible way he had treated Ralph and his family. "Master Terence," she heard him whisper under his breath, peering after the boy.

Orbit snickered. "Hello. Hello. Pretty bird. Clocks-*tick-tock*."

Helena gulped, held Orbit closer to her chest. "That boy. He was throwing pebbles at your door."

"I know," interrupted Mr Westcott. He bent to gather the pebbles from the ground, curling them into his fist so hard that Helena was amazed they didn't crumble into dust.

A lady and gentleman taking an afternoon stroll gave them a lingering and curious glance from underneath their umbrella.

Helena followed Mr Westcott's gaze to the boy's disappearing head. The words which curled from Mr Westcott's lips reminded her of petals falling from flowers. "My poor Boy."

Helena's brain spun in confusion. What did Mr Westcott's daughter have to do with this pebble-throwing child?

Mr Westcott turned and walked back into the house. Helena was about to walk up the steps after him when she noticed that the boy had stopped running, was looking up at an enclosed carriage which had stopped at the side of the road, the horse bowing its head and stamping its hooves as the rain teemed down. She saw a gloved hand appear from a window, and drop something glittery into the boy's open palm. The boy gave a tense and wavering smile to the person in the carriage, balled his hand into a fist and sprinted off, the rain chasing him down the street. *What a curious afternoon*, thought Helena. The mysteries in this house were increasing by the day and she was more determined than ever to solve them.

# CHAPTER 15

# Umbrella

After returning Orbit to his cage, and hanging up her wet jacket to dry, Helena sat back on her heels and rubbed her eyes, wanting nothing more than to lie down, pull the bedspread over her head and think over all the strange things that had happened that day. For some reason, the clocks had stopped when Mr Fox worked here. Her father thought the clock-winding contracts he and Mr Fox had both signed would be null and void if checked over by a solicitor. But, that seemed to be wrong. From what Ralph had told her, Mr Westcott's solicitor had in fact enforced that contract and taken away the Fox family's possessions.

There was a rap on her door. "Helena?" Her father poked his head into the room. "I was beginning to worry you had got lost in the rain! I must have the clock parts you went to collect. One of the table clocks is behaving in a peculiar fashion. Please bring them downstairs at once."

Helena's normally whirring brain was as blank as a wiped-clean school slate as she followed her father. *The clock parts! She had forgotten to go to Regent Street to collect them.* She had been so distracted by her walk into town and from her encounter with Ralph. How to explain she did not have the parts? She did not want to speak of the Fox family to her father – for she knew it would divert him from his job. And it suddenly dawned on her with the clarity of a sunrise what an important job it was. *Their whole livelihood depended on it.*

Helena started at the sight of Boy sitting silently on a chair near the door as she walked into a room lined with tables bearing the weight of carriage and table clocks. She gave Helena a tiny smile. Boy's blonde hair was cut neatly, suggesting the hands of an experienced hairdresser. It made Helena reach up to run her fingers down the length of her own loosely curled ponytail.

What must it feel like to have such short hair? It would be cool in the heat of summer, but chilly in the winter. Did people stop and stare at her on the street, treat her as a curiosity? A thought occurred to her. Perhaps that was why the horrid boy outside had been throwing pebbles at the front door and why Mr Westcott had felt sorry for Boy. Everyone knew that looking different singled a person out from the rest, drew attention when it might not be wanted. Which must mean there was a strong and important reason for Boy to dress differently – a reason she believed in.

"The package please, Helena," her father said, turning to face her.

Helena's mouth felt dry as sand. "Um…I…don't have it," she said, her arms limp by her sides.

Boy's eyes flickered to Helena and stayed there.

Helena's father straightened his back, let out a mountainous sigh. "Why ever not?"

"I…got lost…I mean…I lost the map Stanley drew me…and I couldn't find the clockmaker's shop," Helena added, heat rising up her back.

"How could you possibly get lost? Regent Street is but less than a mile from here. Did you not think to ask a passer-by for directions?" A sudden tightness stretched her father's face into a shape she didn't quite recognize. Helena knew he wanted to throw a few sharp words in her direction, but did not dare because Boy was there observing. She felt Boy's eyes settle on her now. The bud of friendship blooming between them was new and delicate. In Helena's eyes, reliability was an important character trait to seek in a friend and she had just proved herself to be the opposite. A flush of embarrassment warmed her cheeks and she looked at her boots. "I'm sorry, Father. I…I will go tomorrow and collect them."

"That may be too late. It is half an hour until the clock inspection. I just hope Mr Westcott doesn't look too closely at this particular clock. I am disappointed in you, Helena," her father said with a heavy sigh.

Boy stood up abruptly, clattered from the room and went upstairs.

Helena looked after her, wished herself so small she could disappear under the floorboards and away from her father's terrible disappointment.

At ten minutes to six precisely, Mr Westcott stood at the door to the carriage and table-clock room with his sister. Katherine was holding a black umbrella, which was dripping rivulets of water onto the floorboards in the hall. Her jasmine scent wafted into the room ahead of her. "What an unseasonable summer we are having. Now…where is that darling niece of mine?" she said.

"I'm here," said Boy, looking at her father. Helena's eyes widened. Boy's shirt, trousers and boots had been replaced with a cloud-white lacy dress and stockings. A red, satin Alice band pulled her short hair back from her face. Her white leather shoes had been buffed to a high shine.

Mr Westcott glanced at his daughter, his eyes blinking furiously. Then he looked away.

Boy's lips thinned as she continued to stare at her father, her eyes seeking something from him that Helena did not understand.

"Look at your daughter, Edgar. Doesn't she seem well?" Katherine glanced at her brother, who had walked over to the wooden table clock, which Helena's father had said needed a new part. The part she had forgotten to pick up. She bit her bottom lip hard.

Mr Westcott bent his ear to the clock and frowned. "The tick of this clock…it sounds…lighter than normal. It…it…won't stop, will it?" Mr Westcott's cheeks looked as grey as steel.

Katherine sighed loudly, fiddled with the clasp on her umbrella.

"Mr Westcott let me assure you…no clock in this house is in danger of stopping," Helena's father said, the wobble of his chin betraying the confidence in his voice.

Helena swallowed.

"You are certain of this?" Mr Westcott asked, turning his gaze to Helena's father.

Helena's father clasped his hands together and nodded vigorously.

Mr Westcott's eyes had a faraway look in them as he stared at the table clock's unusual face, the series of rings showing the phases of the moon and signs of the zodiac. "It is said that this clock once belonged to Sir Isaac Newton," he murmured.

A gasp of surprise flew from Helena's father's mouth.

"Newton formulated the law of gravity. He was a man of science and logic…attributes to be greatly admired," Mr Westcott whispered. He stood up, turned to face them. His face was bleached of colour. "Please hear me when I say none of the clocks or watches in this house can stop. Ever. If they do…" He paused, rubbed at his neck.

Helena silently willed him to continue. *Why must the clocks not stop?* She just did not understand it. What was Mr Westcott scared of?

"Oh, Edgar…really. Why must we endlessly talk about these clocks of yours?" said Katherine. With a flick of the wrist she opened her umbrella and shook it out, droplets of water scattering like liquid diamonds.

"Katherine!" The shout from Mr Westcott's lips boomed around the room.

Boy leaped backwards.

Helena's father stumbled into a table, shaking the clocks that stood on it.

Helena grabbed her father's arm.

Katherine dropped her umbrella on the floor with a thump.

Mr Westcott strode to his sister and picked up the fallen umbrella, his fingers fumbling to close it.

"I'm…sorry…I didn't…" His sister's cheeks flushed a rosy pink as she struggled to find words to explain herself.

Mr Westcott's eyes were glowering. His grey cheeks had taken on a slightly green hue, as if overcome with seasickness. "Never do that in my house again," he said through gritted teeth, striding from the room, water droplets dripping in his wake from the umbrella.

Boy and Helena exchanged worried glances.

Katherine pulled a handkerchief from her pocket and dabbed at the corners of her watery eyes.

Helena's father took a step towards her. "Do not worry, Miss Westcott. A few water droplets will not damage the clocks."

Katherine pushed her handkerchief up her sleeve, sniffed an elegant sniff and gave Helena's father a thin smile. "It is not the clocks I am worried about," she said tightly, glancing after her brother.

Helena picked up a cloth from her father's toolbox, bent to wipe up the drops of water from the floorboards.

Katherine's forehead crinkled. "No, no, no. Please stop." She beckoned for Helena to stand up. She tipped Helena's chin upwards with a gloved hand. The leather was so soft, Katherine's fingers felt lighter than a whisper on her skin. "Your role in life is not to clean up after others. Do you understand?" Katherine's voice and face were suddenly quite fierce, like a lioness protecting her cubs.

"Um…I'm sorry…yes," Helena said, bunching the cloth into her fist. Whatever did Katherine mean? At home she might not have to do the cooking, but she had taken on her mother's role of washing, changing the sheets and cleaning the floors. How else were things to get done?

"The same applies to you," Katherine said, glancing at Boy, who had scrunched her nose and was looking rather puzzled. Katherine let her fingertips fall from Helena's chin, took the cloth from her hand and bent to wipe up the water herself. She straightened her back and passed the wet cloth to Helena's father, who was clearly unnerved by Katherine's actions. She peeled off her damp gloves and smoothed her skirts. "Right. As my brother is clearly feeling unwell this evening, perhaps you will be so good as to show me the rest of the clocks, Mr Graham?"

Helena's father placed the cloth in his toolbox, clasped his hands together. "Yes...yes of course, Miss Westcott. It would be my pleasure."

"Perhaps we could start...in the longcase-clock room? I would very much like to see the mechanisms, check all is well. I do find it quite fascinating...seeing how they are wound."

Helena's father nodded vigorously and gestured for Katherine to lead the way as the chimes, strikes, bongs and clangs of the clocks marking the hour echoed through the house.

Katherine flashed Helena and Boy a dazzling smile, her skirts swishing like leaves in an autumn wood as she left the room.

*What an odd evening*, Helena thought. Mr Westcott seemed even more erratic in his behaviour. And poor Katherine, how perfectly horrid to have a brother who shouted like that – just because of a little water. Poor Boy too. Could that be why her mother was taking an extended holiday abroad? Perhaps she could help Boy send a message to her mother, tell her she should return home at once. Boy should not be living in this house alone with her father. Helena was beginning to think Mr Westcott was going quite mad.

# CHAPTER 16

# Book Maze

Helena heard the slam of the front door echoing from beneath her window as she got ready for bed. Peeping between her curtains, she watched Mr Westcott step into a carriage, just as he had done a few nights before. She watched the horse clip-clop off into the gloom. Why did he feel the need to go on these night-time trips? Perhaps, if he spent less time going out and more time with Boy, they would both be happier.

Helena kneeled down and unfolded the night cover for Orbit's cage. She stroked her parrot's neck through the bars. "This is rather an unhappy home, Orbit. I fear it is pulling Father away from us…and I don't like it one bit." Orbit snickered gently. "Mother would not have let this happen," whispered Helena.

"Mother loves Helena. Mother loves Helena," said Orbit arching his neck into Helena's fingers. Her mother's bright and breathy laugh filled the small room, squeezing the air from Helena's lungs. She closed her eyes and sat back on her heels, her throat aching. *She and Mother skipping along the pavements to meet Father at his workshop.*

*"People are looking at us," Helena had said breathlessly.*

*"Let them look," her mother had said, her laugh as bright as the sun. "What is the point in being alive if we can't do joyful things like skipping?"*

*Helena had laughed with her, grasped her mother's hand tighter and ignored the tuts and stares from the other pedestrians as they careered along the city streets.*

Helena wiped her eyes on the sleeves of her nightdress, said goodnight to Orbit and gently covered his cage. She placed her arms around it, lay a cheek on the cloth and felt the gentle vibrations of Orbit settling for the night. She had a sudden fierce wish for her father's arms to pull her into an all-encompassing hug and to breathe in the smell of clock oil, which followed him around like a faithful dog. But she did not dare ask him. He would not appreciate such a frivolous request while lost in his mechanical world. It suddenly seemed more urgent than ever to find out where Boy's mother was. She might just hold the key to mending the things that had gone wrong in this strange house. When Boy and *her* father were in the same room, her father behaved as if she wasn't there. Why was that? She wondered whether Boy knew her father had taken away the Fox family's worldly possessions. She somehow thought that if Boy did know the Fox family were heading for the workhouse, she would be as keen to help them as Helena was.

After her father had extinguished his light, Helena crept down the corridor to Boy's bedroom. She paused halfway down, noticing that another flying machine picture had been pinned to the wall beneath a flickering electric light. Although this one was more of a diagram, with all the parts of the machine labelled. *Wings. Propellers. Rudders. Motor.* Who was it intended for? Boy's door was slightly ajar, the light off, but the sound of soft voices spilled from beneath the closed door at the very end of the corridor. Helena crept forward, this time placing her ear against the wooden door, which gave a gentle creak as she leaned against it. There seemed little point in pretending to loiter, catching a word here and there. There were things happening in this house that demanded answers and perhaps being bolder was the only way to find them out.

The door opened with a jolt and she fell into the room, landing on her knees with a thump.

"Oh," she said, heat rising up her back.

Stanley looked down at her. His shirtsleeves were rolled up to his elbows and his face was bright and excited.

"Helena," he said in a hushed voice. "How nice of you to join us." He said it as if she had been invited to a tea party, seemingly unaware of the exceedingly late hour. Except Helena had not received an invitation and there was no tray of cups and slices of cake to be seen.

Helena stood up in a rush, blood pulsing through her head. *She was in a room full of books.* Books placed on top of books lined all four walls, almost to the ceiling. But they weren't only stacked along the walls, they were also placed in shoulder-height rows that marked out the room like a giant chessboard. Helena stood on tiptoes and saw that in the centre there was a space large enough for a small, free-standing blackboard, two chairs and a wooden school desk. Boy was sitting at the desk, her eyebrows raised in surprise.

"Please could you close the door, we don't want to disturb the rest of the house. Come on, mind the books as you walk," said Stanley, gesturing for her to follow him.

Helena quietly clicked the door shut and wound her way through the maze of books to the centre of the room, accidentally nudging a volume or two with her elbow (and desperately yanking them back into place, afraid that if she didn't the whole room would collapse around her, like an over-sized game of dominoes).

Boy was looking up at Stanley expectantly. He had hurried back to the blackboard and now stood in front of it. Written on the board were what looked like rows of mathematical equations in neat cursive handwriting. Scattered on the floor around it were reams of screwed-up balls of paper.

Helena frowned, thinking that the instructions to not speak of unexpected things seen in the house should now be disregarded entirely. "Why…are you giving Boy lessons so late at night?"

Stanley picked up a cloth and wiped the right side of

the blackboard until the equations had vanished. He flapped the cloth, filling the air with clouds of chalk dust.

Helena coughed.

Stanley ignored Helena's question and asked one of his own. "Can you keep a secret? I think you might be able to, or Boy wouldn't trust you quite so much."

Helena glanced at Boy, a small knot of pleasure winding into her. Boy's trust sounded like something valuable and worth having. "Yes...I can keep a secret," she said. Though the only secrets she had been asked to keep before were for things like birthday surprises or Christmas presents. She had a strong sense that the secrets in this house would be quite different. Her palms were slick with perspiration and she wiped them on her nightdress.

Stanley cleared his throat, glanced at Boy.

Boy gave him a small nod.

"As you know, I was employed some months ago by Miss Westcott as a tutor. Teaching Boy is a delight. She displays ability for a wide range of subjects. She's particularly good at the subject of engineering – especially the aeronautical variety which is one of *my* special interests." Stanley gave Boy a proud glance, like a parent would to a child.

Boy smiled a wide-mouthed smile that Helena had not seen before. It changed the shape of her face into something bright and star-like.

Stanley's voice hardened. "Times are difficult in the Westcott household following the departure of the remaining members of staff."

Helena thought of Stanley's well-thumbed copy of *Mrs Beeton's Book of Household Management*. She realized at that moment what an enormous role he had taken on in this house, tutoring Boy and trying to fill in for the staff who had left.

"But I'm determined that despite my other rather unexpected but necessary household duties and the need to keep up with my own studies, Boy shall still receive the education that I was appointed to deliver. She'll achieve wonderful things – just as her aunt wishes." Stanley pointed to the blackboard. "We've been working together in the evenings on the principles of flight. You've heard of the Wright brothers and their flying machines?"

Helena nodded, thinking of the pictures she had found pinned to the walls.

"Just like my father's work with automobiles, this subject, the designing of flying machines, is new and bold. Imagine the wings of a bird. The power and the potential. One day we may all be flying in the air to new places, like your beautiful parrot," said Stanley wistfully.

"But…that…sounds impossible," Helena said. "The Wright brothers have not flown more than two minutes in the air."

"Impossible? Helena, nothing in this world is impossible!" said Stanley. "Imagine if all of the world's greatest inventors had taken that view. Mr Austin and my father believe that one day the automobile will be commonplace and available to everyone. Why not flying machines too? It's well known that small ideas turn impossibilities into possibilities."

Helena stared at him, letting the words sink into her brain. She turned to Boy, walked over to her desk. "The drawings of the Wright brothers' flying machines I keep finding. You drew them, didn't you?"

"Yes," Boy said, chewing on the end of her pencil.

"They are truly very good. But why pin them to the walls?" asked Helena.

Boy glanced at Stanley.

"Boy's drawings show a lot of potential. But Mr Westcott's not open to potential at the moment. In fact, he's not open to many things at all," Stanley said, his voice tight with disapproval.

Helena remembered how Boy had looked up at her father expectantly during the clock inspections, and how he always gravitated towards the clocks rather than his daughter. *Boy is putting the drawings on the wall to get her father's attention,* thought Helena. *How very sad.*

Boy bent her head and began shading the wing of a flying machine. "We have written a letter to the Wright brothers," she said. "We think we've engineered a way to make their machines stay in the air for longer."

"But…how?" asked Helena. It did sound impossible. How could a young tutor and a twelve-year-old girl know more than two of the world's most famous inventors?

"I'll be studying mechanical sciences at Cambridge University from September," said Stanley, a flush creeping up his neck. "I'll be the first in my family to go to university, something my parents are still a little flummoxed about and don't entirely agree with. My father learned his trade while working, but I want to learn about the theory of things, properly understand how machines work. Flight is one of my many areas of interest and it seems I've passed this interest on to Boy.

Miss Westcott is impressed with our discoveries and she's fully supportive of our efforts." His voice swelled with pride.

Helena's eyes widened. She remembered Stanley telling her that he had taken the position in this house because of the books that could help him with his own studies. He was not only a tutor; he was about to attend one of the most famous universities in the world, which also meant he was extraordinarily clever. Her admiration for him grew even stronger.

But while Stanley and Boy worked on their ambitious plans, all Helena could think of was the plight of the Fox family because of Mr Westcott's actions, and the threat Helena and her father had hanging over their heads. Helena felt a muscle twitch in her left eye. She needed to find out if Boy knew the reasons behind her father's unjustified behaviour. But to tell Boy the whole truth about the signed contract would mean that she was breaking Mr Westcott's rule. If he found out she had told Stanley and Boy about the contract, she could say goodbye to Orbit and the remainder of their possessions. Stanley said that Boy trusted her. But could she trust Boy?

# CHAPTER 17

# Mechanical Parts

"No, my father would not have done that," Boy said, pushing her chair back so it toppled into a pile of books. Books pushed over books, pushing over more books that landed on the floor in a heap.

"Oh, watch it," said Stanley, stumbling forward to rescue them. "Stop. You'll wake the house!"

"My father would not have taken another family's possessions. He would not make Mr Fox or your father sign such a contract," said Boy, ignoring Stanley's plea for quiet.

Stanley's attempts to prevent more books from

falling were only increasing the domino effect as they cascaded onto the floor one after another.

"But he has," Helena said simply.

Boy folded her arms. "You don't know my father. He is a good person."

Helena's skin bristled. *But he isn't. Not really,* thought Helena. *Why can't Boy see that?* "Your mother is in France. Your father is horrid to your aunt. He ignores you – and your drawings. What's going on, Boy?"

Boy pressed her lips together and did not argue back, which made Helena certain she was keeping more secrets.

Helena gestured around the room, at the stacks of books. "These books should be on shelves in the library, not stacked in here to make space for the clocks. Why is your father so obsessed with keeping the clocks ticking?"

Stanley was still picking up the books, muttering under his breath.

Boy bent to pick up a couple of books, while chewing on her bottom lip.

Heat bloomed in Helena's chest, and she turned and clambered and slipped and slid over the books to the door. She had been wrong to think that Boy could be an ally. She just hoped that Boy would not run to her father or aunt and repeat what Helena had told her about the clock-winding contracts. If she did, she and her father would be in the most tremendous trouble.

Helena paced up and down in her room. Boy did not believe that her father had drawn up the contracts or taken the Foxes's things. She could not let that poor family end up in the workhouse as a result of Mr Westcott's terrible actions. And she had to make sure her father did not allow the very same thing to happen to them, which meant she needed to find some answers.

Pulling on her cardigan, Helena opened her bedroom door. She tiptoed down the moonlit stairs, the ticks and tocks of the clocks smothering the occasional creaks of the floorboards.

She began her search in the pocket-watch room, opening each and every watch in case secret compartments were concealing more hidden messages.

She crept into the room of longcase clocks, stood in front of the moon-faced pendulum bob clock, which Mr Westcott had seemed particularly taken with. The room was as cold as a tomb and just about as welcoming. She rubbed her nose. The clock seemed vaguely familiar, but the thought zipped away from her like trying to catch a fish. The pendulum bob swung creepily in the darkness, the cherubic moon-face returning her stare. The clocks began to strike the half hour, making Helena jump. She did not think she would ever grow used to the chimes and strikes. They echoed uncomfortably in her head long after finishing, like an unwelcome conversation that had lasted too long. She pressed a hand to her fast-beating heart as the noise faded. She needed to hurry. It would not do to be caught by Mr Westcott after he returned from his mysterious night-time wanderings. On the ground floor she paused outside Mr Westcott's study door. There was no blade of light coming from beneath it and she had not heard him return from wherever he had been. Where did he go to at night? She placed a hand on the doorknob and gave it a tentative turn. It was locked of course.

"Helena?"

Helena whirled round, her hand flying to her mouth. *Stanley.* "I was just…I was just…" she gasped, her heart thumping hard against her ribs.

Stanley held a pencil in his hand. "I was studying in the kitchen and I heard a noise. Can't you sleep?" he said.

Helena shook her head as her heart slowed to a steady beat.

"Come on, I'll warm us some milk. That's what my mother used to do on the nights I couldn't settle." Stanley flashed Helena a quick smile, turned and disappeared down the basement stairs.

Helena glanced at one of the longcase clocks. Stanley was studying at eleven o'clock in the evening, when most people were in bed sound asleep. A short while ago he had been teaching Boy equations and talking about flying machines in a book-filled room. A dark cloud of weariness suddenly bowed Helena's shoulders at all the odd goings-on in the house. With a small sigh she followed him.

Stanley stood at the range warming milk in a copper pan. He stirred the milk with a wooden spoon, swirling it in hypnotic circles.

Helena leaned against the wall. The kitchen table was piled high with leather-bound books and sheets of paper filled with neat handwriting. She thought of Stanley's hard-earned place at Cambridge University and his role tutoring Boy so he could earn enough money to support himself. "Why do you do *all* of the cooking and look after the house, Stanley? Why try so

hard to please Mr Westcott, especially as he is so…
unappreciative of your efforts?"

Stanley smiled as he looked down at the milk. "This
must all seem a bit strange to you and your father."

Helena nodded.

Stanley turned to look at her. "Automobiles and
flying machines are made up of many different
mechanical parts. Sometimes those parts get broken
and need fixing. My mother often says people are the
same as machines…they can sometimes need a bit of
fixing too."

"Are you talking about…Mr Westcott. And Boy?"
said Helena.

Stanley nodded, lifted the pan off the range as the
milk began to rise and poured it into two tin mugs.

"But you heard me telling Boy about the contract Mr
Westcott made my father sign…and what has happened
to the Fox family. Mr Westcott is not nice at all…he is
bitter…and horrid and…he keeps going out at night
and…" said Helena.

"Ah, but," interrupted Stanley. "Sometimes it
doesn't pay to decide on a person's character or
circumstances until you know them better. There are
reasons people behave the way they do, reasons that

often become clear over time. Mr Westcott has treated the Fox family poorly, but there may be a reason for his behaviour."

"Well, I certainly can't think of a good reason why Mr Westcott prefers his clocks to his own daughter and has treated the Fox family so terribly," said Helena, taking a mug from Stanley and blowing on the warm milk.

Stanley drank his milk, looking at Helena steadily. "I'm a little unsure of what it will be like when I start at the university. I imagine the other students might be different to me, have had advantages in life that I haven't been privy to. But I see now that even those who've had advantages, like the Westcott family, can still have troubled lives. Mr Westcott has an odd kind of sadness behind his eyes. I see it in his daughter's eyes too. But it's not my business to pry into their affairs – I do the job I am paid for, and try and help while I am here." Stanley gave Helena a small smile. "Isn't that what anyone would do if they saw folks who needed a helping hand?"

Helena nodded, remembering all of the small kindnesses she and her father had received after her mother had died. The hot meals, the offers of washing and help with the cleaning. Stanley was right. Maybe she needed to be a little more understanding.

"I've enjoyed talking to you this evening, Helena. But I must go to bed – I've lots to do in the morning." The skin under Stanley's eyes was pinched with tiredness. He was working all hours of the day and night for a family who didn't seem much like a family at all.

"I will wash up the mugs and milk pan when I've finished," Helena said.

"Oh no…I can do it," protested Stanley.

"I insist," said Helena firmly. "Now go…please. It will not take me a minute."

"Well, if you're sure," said Stanley gratefully.

"Absolutely sure," Helena said with a smile.

Helena dried her hands on a cloth and turned to look at the tidy kitchen. She stifled a yawn. It had been a long and surprising day and she was ready for bed. As she turned to leave, a quiver of light illuminated the kitchen then vanished.

Helena frowned, turning to look at the dark panes of glass.

The sound of feet crunching on gravel.

Someone was outside in Mr Westcott's garden – with a lantern.

Helena stood on tiptoes at the basement window. She was not tall enough to see out to the garden above. *Was it Mr Westcott? If he had returned from wherever he had been, why was he now in the garden at night?* Stanley had seemed unconcerned by Mr Westcott's night-time wanderings. Maybe, if she followed him, she would discover the reason for his strange behaviour.

# CHAPTER 18

# Postcard

Unlocking and opening the back door, Helena crept up the stone steps to Mr Westcott's garden and peered across the moonlit grass. It was the first time she had been in the garden, having only previously seen it from the upstairs windows. The moon bathed the foliage in a soft white light and the trees rustled and waved as if saying hello. A lone rabbit hopped about in the shadows. She was glad of its company as her eyes followed the pinprick of light which was moving close to the garden wall. Keeping to the shadows, Helena dashed up the remaining steps and ran through the too-long grass, which tickled her bare ankles. The point of light suddenly became brighter and was then gone, as if swallowed up by a giant's mouth. She skirted around a forlorn stone fountain with no water, past a wooden bench with strips of peeling paint hanging off it like skin. Her heart kicked hard in her chest as she ducked behind a row of trees. Hidden from the house was a single-storey brick building – an old stable. There were no horses now, though, just a small cobbled courtyard and three stable doors. The top half of one door was ajar, a light flickering inside. Helena sidled up to the half-closed door and crouched beneath it. Bumps and thumps were coming from inside the stable. A sudden thought occurred to her. Was this where Mr Westcott was storing the Foxes's things? Maybe she should confront him and insist he return their possessions at once! The thought of his piercing sapphire eyes made Helena shiver and she hurriedly swallowed the thought.

*Clunk.* "Bother it," whispered a voice.

Helena froze. A familiar jasmine scent drifted over the stable door and prickled her nose. *Katherine Westcott.* Helena's hands felt clammy and hot all at once.

"Where are they?" Katherine muttered. The scent of

jasmine was growing stronger. She was approaching the half-closed door.

Helena dragged in a silent breath and scurried around the side of the building, cowering near a large upside-down plant pot.

More clunking and dragging of objects across the floor. *What was Katherine Westcott doing?*

Then the sound of the door shutting. Katherine Westcott's back retreated into the dark, the lantern swinging from her right arm.

Helena slunk after her, once more keeping to the shadows of the high brick wall which separated Mr Westcott's garden from his neighbours. She paused, watched Katherine go past the house and down a passage which led to Trumpington Street. The side gate was open, the glow of the streetlamps on the road throwing a blade of light down the passageway. Helena heard the snort of a horse, saw a carriage waiting. She leaned back against the wall, the brick cool and crumbly against her palms. Katherine Westcott was creeping around her brother's garden at night. And as far as Helena could see, people only slunk around in the dark when they were doing things they wanted to hide.

Helena woke to a tremendous sucking, bumping noise coming from the rooms below her bedroom.

"Hickory-dickory-*squawk*," cried Orbit from under his night cover.

She jumped out of bed and pulled back the curtains. It was only a little after seven-thirty in the morning, yet a small crowd of onlookers had gathered on the pavement outside Mr Westcott's house.

Stanley was standing on the steps, a broad grin on his face as he directed a red-uniformed man standing on a ladder holding a thick hose. Helena's eyes followed the length of the hose – to a red horse-drawn van with the letters BVCC on the side. *The British Vacuum Cleaner Company.*

There was an urgent rap at her door and Helena's father burst in, his face lit up. "Mr Westcott has appointed one of Booth's cleaning vans to come and extract the dust from the clock rooms. Quick, Helena! We must be present to make sure they are not damaged. I have heard great things about this machine – can you believe it – a machine, which can remove the dust from rooms! Whoever would have imagined such a thing?"

Throwing on her dress and only half-lacing her boots, Helena ran downstairs.

Boy was standing at the entrance to the longcase-clock room, a look of enchantment on her face. "Have you ever seen anything like it?" she whispered to Helena, the difficult words they had exchanged the night before seemingly forgotten. "Stanley saw an advertisement in one of the London papers for this machine. When Father saw it, he said it must be brought to Cambridge immediately to clean the clock rooms."

Another red-uniformed man was in the clock room directing the end of the hose through the open window, where it sucked and slurped at the floorboards (as far as Helena could see they were pretty spotless already).

"Mind the clocks! Mind the clocks!" shouted Helena's father, who was flapping about the room like a mother hen, strategically placing himself between the clocks and the hose.

Helena could feel a giggle bubbling in her throat.

A chuckle flew from Boy's lips.

They glanced at one another and Helena grinned. "No. I've never seen anything so bizarre in my whole life."

Boy's smile dropped a little and she rubbed her nose. "What you said last night...I just find it hard to believe my father could do something so…horrid," she said quietly.

Helena stood a little closer to Boy, until their arms were touching. "I'm sorry, Boy. But what I said is the truth."

Boy pushed her hands into her trouser pockets. "Will you come with me? I want to show you something."

Helena nodded and followed Boy into the pocket-watch room next door. Boy closed the door and went to stand by the window. She pulled out a piece of card from her pocket and held it out to Helena. It was a postcard. On the front was a drawing of a lady on a hill holding a ruby-red parasol. She gazed through palm trees down to an aquamarine sea. On the top of the card in swirly white writing it said: *Hotel Imperial, Côte d'Azur*. Helena turned it over to read the words on the back.

*12th May 1905*
*My darlings,*

*I very much hope to be home next month! I have missed you both so much and am at last beginning to gain strength. I am thinking of you all the time and I do not want you to worry about a thing. I cannot wait*

*until we are all reunited. I will write again soon to let*
*you know my travel arrangements.*
*With fondest love,*
*Mother*

"I have not heard from Mother since this last postcard arrived three weeks and two days ago," said Boy miserably. "I wait for the post to arrive every day and…there is no word."

"But your father must be terribly worried. Has he not said anything?" asked Helena.

"I want to talk to him about it, but Aunt Katherine said I should not worry him. She says…he hasn't been feeling well," said Boy.

Helena handed the card back to Boy. It was creased at the edges and on the folds, like it had been pored over many times.

"Is your mother's name Evangeline?" asked Helena, remembering Mr Westcott's mutterings from one of the clock rooms a few nights before.

Boy frowned. "Why?"

"Two nights ago, when Orbit escaped…I overheard your father say that name," said Helena. "He said your name too."

"So, he does think about her," said Boy, her eyes brightening a little.

"But of course, he must! When someone is not here any more, you don't just stop remembering them," Helena said firmly.

"But it feels like Mother's vanished into thin air," sighed Boy.

"Why *did* she go to France?" asked Helena. "She says in the card she is gaining strength."

"She went to a health spa," said Boy, turning to look out of the window.

"Was she...is she...ill?" Helena asked. *Was Boy's mother sick, just as her mother had been?*

"Not exactly," said Boy, folding the card and putting it into her pocket.

Helena sighed. Talking to Boy was like doing an awkward dance – one step forward and two back. "Perhaps we could go into town to the post office, send a telegram to the hotel?"

"Stanley helped me to do that already," said Boy. "We received a reply saying she had left. There was no forwarding address."

"Oh," said Helena, wrinkling her nose. *How peculiar. And how worrying.*

"Here you are," said Stanley, rushing into the room. In his hands was a wicker basket. "For the Fox family," he said, nodding at the basket. "Would you be able to do me a favour and deliver these provisions to the Fox family? Please tell them I'm very sorry for their hardship and would like to help in any way I can. Mr Fox is a good man." He pushed the basket into Helena's hands. "Please give Mr Fox my regards and tell him I am... sorry."

Helena clenched the basket handle tightly, hoping against hope that the family were not already consigned to the workhouse.

"You believe it was my father's fault...that the Fox family lost their things?" asked Boy in a small voice.

"Yes, I do," Stanley said gently. "But as I was telling Helena just last night, there'll be a reason behind his actions. I don't believe your father is a cruel man."

Boy stood up a little straighter, pushed her hands into her trouser pockets. "Then I will go to Mr Fox's with Helena."

Stanley's face contorted in alarm. "But...you haven't been outside in weeks...are you sure...?"

"I should see for myself what my father has done to this family," Boy said firmly.

Helena gave Boy a small smile, thankful that she had changed her mind. They would pay a quick visit to the Fox family, and she would be able to collect the clock parts she had forgotten the day before, which would please her father. But her jaw tightened at the thought of what they might find when they arrived at Mr Fox's shop and what Boy's reaction would be when she learned the true implications of her father's terrible and unjustified behaviour. She felt a little scared but knew this was no time to be faint-hearted. She just hoped that visiting Mr Fox would lead them one step further to finding out the truth.

# CHAPTER 19

# Bridge

They must look an odd pair, Helena thought, as she and Boy walked towards the town centre. A girl dressed as a boy, carrying a parrot in a bag, and a girl carrying a basket loaded with provisions.

Orbit's eyes were bright, his head swivelling at the sights and sounds: stuttering automobiles with men and ladies in fine dresses and gauzy hats, students in short sleeves on bicycles, whistling birds in the trees, their voices throwing threads of silver into the air.

"Pretty Mother, Humpty Dumpty, all fall down," Orbit squawked, as a lady with a large cream hat decorated with blood-red berries walked past. The lady turned, gave Orbit, Helena and Boy a stare, and covered her open mouth with a gloved hand.

Helena stifled a giggle.

Boy smiled, her cheeks broad as they breathed in the apple-fresh air.

They continued along Trumpington Street, past a buttery coloured stone building, which gave Helena the impression of a small castle with its crenellated walls and arched windows. "Is this a university college too, like Peterhouse?" Helena asked Boy, peering at a carved stone crest above an open doorway.

A man in a top hat, standing at the entrance, overheard. "This is Pembroke College, Miss," he said, puffing up his chest a little like Orbit did when he was trying to impress. "It has educated some of the finest people of our country, including our youngest-ever Prime Minister, Mr William Pitt the Younger, who was only twenty-four. What's more, a little over one hundred years ago, he helped lead Britain in the wars against Napoleon and France."

Helena nodded her thanks to the man. Perhaps these colleges were castles of sorts – strongholds to keep the students hidden from the outside world while they learned great and important things, allowing them to *do* great and important things later in life. She thought of Stanley's ambitions to study in Cambridge and assist the Wright brothers with their inventions, his worries about being different to the other students. With his determination and concern for others, he deserved a good future.

"Why are you so interested in the Wright brothers?" Helena asked Boy, as they crossed Pembroke Street.

"Do you really want to know?" said Boy, giving Orbit's crown a gentle stroke.

"Well, I don't know much about science – and Father is always a little disappointed at the results I get in Miss Granger's Mathematics exams – but I am interested, yes. Your drawings are really quite brilliant," said Helena.

A flush stole onto Boy's cheeks. "I've never been to school, but I had a governess before Mother left. She certainly wasn't very interested in teaching me anything useful, but Stanley is...well...I've never met anyone like him before. His parents might not understand the future he's chosen for himself, but he's pursuing it anyway. I admire that." Boy suddenly stopped, held out her arms like wings. "You need three things in order to fly. Lift, forward thrust and control. The Wright brothers have been trying to use these principles to make their flying machines take to the air. But so far they have not been too successful. Stanley and I have been studying the designs of the machines, looking at their individual parts. We think that if the Wright brothers moved the rudder further away from the wings, this would allow the pilot to have increased control, allow their machines to stay in the air for longer."

"But...however did you work that out?" asked Helena, scrunching her nose.

"I think when someone like Stanley is teaching you interesting things, it is easier to come up with interesting ideas," said Boy, her eyes glinting. "And it wasn't all me...Stanley invented most of it. He's been talking to people at the university – they are excited about it too. As is Aunt Katherine. I think I should like to go to university one day, perhaps to study mechanical sciences."

"I wish I was good at something," said Helena. While she was happy for Boy, she was also slightly envious. What must it be like to have found something you enjoyed and excelled in?

165

"Do you go to school?" asked Boy.

Helena nodded.

Boy frowned. "I can't imagine being taught in a proper classroom with other children. I'd quite like to try it."

Helena thought of her high-windowed classroom, the glare from the sun in summer, the frosts, which patterned the inside of the glass in winter, the coughs and colds that passed from child to child like a game of tag and the mistress's desk at the front with the dreaded cane resting on top of it, encouraging obedience at all times. Then she thought of the maze of books on the top floor of Boy's house, and Stanley's determination to learn. "I wouldn't try and imagine what school is like too much – you are lucky to have Stanley tutoring you... I wonder if the Wright brothers will reply to your letter?" mused Helena, walking on. "Just think, Boy. They might invite you to go to America..." She paused. Boy had lagged behind. Her flying machine arms had dropped to her sides and she was staring ahead, the shine gone from her eyes.

"Oh," Helena said in dismay, looking at a cart which had shed its load of coal at the junction of Trumpington Street and Silver Street.

"You'll have to go along Silver Street, cross the bridge and go along The Backs if you want to get into town," called a man in blackened overalls who was directing the traffic, while another shovelled the coal back into the cart.

"The Backs?" Helena called.

"Along the river," said Boy in a low voice.

"Oh, how lovely," said Helena brightly. "I haven't seen the river yet. I should like to see the boats."

Helena hurried down Silver Street, with Boy trailing behind a little, until the buildings on each side fell away to reveal a bridge. Groups of men and women were sitting in long and narrow square-ended, flat-bottomed boats – which she soon learned were called punts. The men standing at the back of each punt forced long wooden poles against the riverbed to propel the boats forwards. Along the riverbank, willow trees dipped their lacy fingers into the sparkling water, while the ladies in the punts rested blankets over their knees and wicker picnic baskets at their feet, brimming with clear glass bottles of pop, bottles of champagne and cake tins. Their laughs and shouts carried across the water and Helena leaned over the bridge, drinking in the scene with greedy eyes. She was suddenly aware of the quietness behind her. The lack of footsteps, squawks and singing from Orbit.

She turned. Boy was standing stock still on the other side of the bridge. Orbit was pulled close to her chest, as if she were trying to protect him from something. Her eyes were wide, but not with wonder. With fear.

Helena swung the basket onto her arm and ran back across the bridge. "Whatever is the matter?" she asked, her heart hammering against her ribs. She glanced behind her, half expecting to see an axe-wielding man running towards them, but instead saw other hurrying pedestrians, a man pushing a handcart, cycling students and hansom cabs pulled by clattering horses.

Boy's eyes were still fixed straight ahead. Her hands shook as she held Orbit.

"Hickory-dickory," squawked the bird, his eyes blinking.

Helena swallowed, reached forward and gently prised Orbit from Boy's trembling hands.

Boy clearly could not tell Helena what was wrong, and Helena sensed that now was not the time to question *why* Boy was afraid. She was beginning to realize that asking the first questions that popped into her head may not always be the best approach. Stanley was right that there was always a reason behind a person's behaviour. Perhaps it was better to let people speak in their own time. But they did need to cross the bridge over the river to get to Rose Crescent to deliver the food to the Fox family and collect the clock parts for her father.

"Come," Helena said, holding out her hand.

Boy looked at her, a muscle in her jaw twitching.

"There's really nothing to be afraid of. Orbit and I are here," said Helena.

Boy blinked and blinked, as if she was washing away the fears which had frozen her to the wrong side of the bridge.

"We will find another way back to the house if the coal is still blocking the road. It will be all right, Boy. I promise."

With an almost imperceptible nod, Boy slipped her hand into Helena's and allowed herself to be led over the river. The trust Boy was placing in her made Helena push her shoulders back and resolve to do her utmost to somehow put right the things that had gone so very wrong for the Westcott family.

# CHAPTER 20

# Mr Fox

The bell jangled as Helena opened the door to Mr Fox's shop. A man with extraordinarily bushy sideburns was sweeping the floor. Ralph and his two sisters were sitting on the shop counter, bumping their feet against the wood.

"Pa," exclaimed Ralph. "This is the girl I was telling you about. The one with the parrot. From Mr Westcott's house." He jumped down from the counter and ran across to them, eyeing the basket Helena was carrying with interest.

Mr Fox leaned the brush against the counter and

wiped his hands on his trousers. "You," he said, pointing at Boy. "You would sit in the clock rooms while I worked sometimes."

Boy gave him a cautious nod.

"This is…Mr Westcott's daughter," Helena said.

Mr Fox's eyes narrowed and he sucked in a sharp breath. "You have some nerve coming to visit us here after what your father has done to my family…"

Helena sensed Boy stiffen beside her.

"Oh no, Mr Fox," Helena said, grabbing Boy's hand before she could run out of the shop. "She knew nothing of what her father did."

"Is that true?" Mr Fox said gruffly.

Boy bravely looked him in the eye and nodded. She pulled away from Helena's grasp. Her eyes were fierce and brimming with fire. "Tell me everything my father has done. Don't spare me the terrible parts. If his character is truly not what I thought it to be, then I need to know. And I promise I will do everything I can to help you."

Helena was prepared for the bare floorboards, walls and the absence of furniture in the rooms above the shop.

Boy wasn't. Helena watched the girl's gaze settle on spots on the walls where pictures would have hung, the space in front of the fireplace where a rug would have covered the floorboards, the window seat missing a cushion.

"My father…did this?" Boy said in a small voice.

Mr Fox gave her a curt nod. "I know he is your father, but that man has a lot to answer for."

Boy's face crumpled like a handkerchief clutched into a fist, as she slowly walked around the room taking in the absence of everything one would expect to find in a home.

Orbit wriggled and squawked, his bag swinging from Helena's shoulder.

"You found my card inside the pocket watch," Mr Fox said, looking at Helena. "I hoped that the new clockmaker might examine that watch, as it is a rare one. I wanted to warn whoever was appointed to the position after me. I am sorry it was too late."

"But it's not too late," said Helena. "The clocks have not stopped for my father."

"Yet," said Mr Fox grimly.

Helena's stomach turned. "We really cannot lose our things…if I lose my parrot…"

Mr Fox gently stroked Orbit's head. The parrot snickered and bobbed and swayed his head from side to side. Ralph's sisters giggled.

"You can let your parrot out of his bag, if you like?" Mr Fox said. "The windows are shut. My sister had a parakeet. Great escape artist it was, could even unlock his own cage."

"Orbit is the same," Helena said, loosening the strings of the bag and letting him flap free. "One time, he flew out of the kitchen window, over the garden wall and onto the neighbours' washing line. You can imagine what happened next."

Mr Fox wrinkled his nose.

"Exactly. I had to re-wash Mrs Berkeley's bloomers. It was horrid. Father bought a lock and key for the cage after that. Orbit hasn't escaped since."

Orbit stretched his wings wide, bowed his head as if in thanks and walked round in a circle, his feet clicking on the wooden boards. Helena's mother's laugh tinkled from his beak.

"Why, what a perfectly wonderful laugh," said Mr Fox, rubbing his sideburns. "Your bird mimics you well."

Helena felt as if a kaleidoscope of butterflies had

flown into her stomach. Mr Fox did not need to know that the laugh which came from Orbit's beak did not belong to her.

Ralph's youngest sister giggled again and came to stand next to Helena.

"Here, I've brought you some food from Stanley," Helena said, passing Mr Fox the basket. "He sends his regards."

Nibbling on a thumbnail, Boy walked over. She had been looking at the faded outline on the wall where a picture had once hung.

"Stanley has provided us with a feast," said Mr Fox, peering inside the picnic basket. "Take it to your ma," he said gently to his eldest daughter. "Tell her there are two more for an early lunch. We shall eat at once."

"Oh no," Boy said. "That food is for you."

"I am not so bitter at my misfortune that I am unable to share the little I have," Mr Fox said firmly. "You are our guests and I shall hear no more of it. We shall eat here. Fetch the blanket, will you, Ralph?"

A blue and yellow checked blanket was laid in front of the fireplace (Ralph had borrowed it from the publican next door). An assortment of chipped plates and knives and forks (which Mr Fox said had been

174

loaned by the owners of the cobblers across the crescent) were used to dish up slices of ham, crumbly cheese, a crusty loaf of bread and an assortment of apples.

"You have good neighbours," said Boy, glancing at Ralph and his sisters as they sat cross-legged on the rug, their eyes bright as they chewed.

Mrs Fox entered the room quietly and joined them on the blanket, where she sat dull-eyed, throwing Boy and Helena suspicious glances. "They won't be our neighbours for much longer," she said under her breath.

"I am…truly sorry for your troubles," said Boy, her voice cracking a little. She passed Ralph's mother a plate of food.

Mrs Fox looked at her for a few seconds. Her steely eyes softened a little. "Thank you," she muttered.

"The clocks, then," Helena said, pushing away the heaviness in her chest and feeding Orbit a handful of seeds. "Why do *you* think they stopped, Mr Fox?"

Mr Fox forked a slice of ham into his mouth and chewed thoughtfully. "I know my trade. Every cog and wheel and spring in Mr Westcott's clocks was in perfect working order."

"So how could they have stopped?" asked Boy, her nose wrinkling.

"Human interference," said Mr Fox firmly.

"But…who would do that?" asked Helena. "Does that mean it will happen again, to my father?"

Boy glanced at Helena, then looked down at the bread and cheese on her plate.

"I don't know. But the person responsible is someone who knows about clocks," Mr Fox said, shooting Boy a quick look. "Mr Westcott was quite bright the morning the clocks stopped, his cheeks less grey than usual. He spoke to me about the clocks, praised me for my work before he left the house. I was there all day – working on the second floor. When Mr Westcott returned to the house that evening, he was like a changed man. His eyes were wild – like a storm over the Fens. It was during the clock inspection that I noticed some of the longcase clocks on the ground floor had stopped. I had not been in that room all day. Mr Westcott's face when he found out…well…" Mr Fox paused, rubbed his nose as if trying to erase the memory. "Later that evening, a man and a young boy arrived at my shop with a cart and took away our possessions. Every day since I've been at Marchington's

– Mr Westcott's solicitors – begging them to return our belongings. I sense some sympathy from them, but anyone would think their lips had been sealed with glue. We need to get them unsealed quickly, or I'm afraid it will be the workhouse for us."

Boy stood up, brushed the crumbs from her trousers. She tucked her hair behind her ears. "I will help you get your things back, Mr Fox. I promise. And I will find out why my father is behaving so terribly. You are right, something must be done, and Helena and I will be the ones to do it."

Helena stared at Boy. Her eyes were even more fiery now than when they had first arrived. She swallowed hard at a piece of bread that seemed to be wedged in her throat, and a thought suddenly occurred to her. Was Boy upset because of what her father had done – or was there another reason? Mr Fox said the clocks had been stopped by human hands. Boy had pinned drawings to the walls, desperate for her father to notice her. Had she done something else to get her father's attention that she now regretted? She was always in the clock rooms. Helena took a sip of water, swallowed again, her appetite suddenly lost. The thought was almost too awful to acknowledge, but maybe the quiet desperation she sensed in Boy had pushed her into doing something dreadful, and the answer to the stopped clocks had been right under her nose all along.

# CHAPTER 21

# Dr Barrington

Helena bit her lip in concentration as she used a miniature brush to clean the sails of a windmill, which, when the hour chimed, rocked a ship on small wooden waves and rolled a figure out of the doors of a church. Her mind kept wandering to Boy and the Fox family and she realized with a start that in her distraction she had cleaned the windmill sails twice over. When she had finished, she carefully replaced the glass dome on the automaton clock, giving it a final polish with her dress sleeve.

Boy sat in her usual position by the door. Her face

was set into a shape Helena had not seen in all the five days she had been in Cambridge. It was as if her features were paint colours and had been swirled around in a glass of water. The tips of her ears were pink. Her blue eyes were brighter than ever and glassy. Her cheeks were as flushed as the tips of her ears. Boy had been talkative as they walked from Mr Fox's shop to Regent's Street to pick up the forgotten clock parts from the previous day. *Where could my father have taken the Foxes's things? What would he want with them? Why hasn't my mother come home? Do you think my father is ill?*

Helena had not had any answers to Boy's questions and so stayed silent, scuffing her boots along the pavement, as the sunny start to the day was shrouded with cloud and a light drizzle. Had Boy stopped the clocks? She had not known about the clock contracts, so would not have realized the implications her actions would have. Was that why her eyes had been so full of fire after leaving the Fox family, why she was so determined to help?

"My dear girls," said Katherine, sweeping into the room in a cornflower-blue coat a little before six o'clock that evening. In her arms she held a green box about the size of Boy's chair seat. It was tied up with a red ribbon. She placed it on Boy's lap. "For you," she said, bending to drop a light kiss on the top of Boy's head. As usual, Boy had changed before the clock inspection, discarding her boy's outfit for a midnight-blue pleated skirt and cream blouse with a lace collar. Helena thought that Boy seemed more at ease with herself when she dressed like this, as if this was her true self. But if that was the case, who was she trying to please when she dressed in boys' clothes? Her eyes were locked to the gift. Oh, to have a beautiful aunt who bought presents and dispensed kisses like sweets. She had an uncle on her mother's side, who did not visit often, and her father was an only child just as she was. Helena squashed the jolt of envy under the heels of her boots.

A flush stole onto Boy's cheeks. She slowly pulled at the ribbon around the box, letting it drift to the floor near the heels of her aunt's shoes. Miss Westcott's heels were thick with mud. The hems of her long coat had a slightly dark tinge to them too. Helena frowned, remembering Katherine's curious visit to the stables the night before, when she was not even a guest in the house.

Peeling back layers of wafer-thin tissue paper, Boy

pulled out two hardback books. Helena's fingers tingled with disappointment. She had been expecting a pretty dress, or maybe a pair of beaded slippers. She peered at the titles.

*A History of Architecture*

*The Problem of Manflight*

Boy smiled broadly, stood up and gave her aunt a quick hug.

Katherine's eyes sparkled. "Make sure you read every word, darling niece. You never know where they may lead you." She turned and Helena gulped at the sight of her hat. She had thought it to be a quite plain sky-blue felted hat, but now saw one side was decorated with peacock-feather eyes, which stared back at Helena in a disconcerting way. "There will be no clock inspection this evening. My brother…decided he felt unwell when I arrived," she said, a frown straining her features which made her look rather weary.

"Well…if you're quite sure…" said Helena's father.

"Yes, quite sure," Katherine said, bending over Orbit's cage. "Hello birdy, birdy, birdy," she said, tapping on the bars.

"*Squawk-squawk-squawk,*" screeched Orbit, crouching and swaying from side to side.

"Oh." Katherine gave a tinkling laugh. "I do declare this bird is rather fond of me."

Fluffing his back feathers, Orbit launched forward, the nip of his beak narrowly missing Katherine's gloved finger.

With another laugh and a small shake of her head, Katherine threw Helena and Boy one last dazzling smile, turned and swept from the room.

Helena's father was already packing his tools away. "An early night will be most welcome," he said. "I am quite exhausted. Looking after all these clocks is rather more work than I had anticipated, and that's with your assistance, my dear Helena. Thank you for collecting the clock parts – I am sorry I was so hard on you yesterday…"

But Helena wasn't listening. She was looking at the mysterious swooping wet stains on the wooden floor left by Katherine's damp coat, and the chunks of mud from her shoes. And why did Orbit screech and become so aggressive whenever she approached him?

A low murmur of voices was coming from the hall. Helena glanced at Boy, but she was engrossed in one of her new books, her eyes eagerly scanning the pages.

Helena sidled to the door, peered around the frame.

"You must take your hat from this house, Katherine. I cannot bear it," said Mr Westcott in a low voice. His face was a pallid smoky-grey.

"But…that is quite irrational of you, Edgar," Katherine said, adjusting the brim of her hat.

Mr Westcott flinched, grabbed on to the bannister to steady himself. "I fear…I fear…I cannot take much more of this."

"I know, my dear. And that is why you have an appointment to see Dr Barrington tomorrow."

"Dr Barrington?" Mr Westcott said, his eyes widening. "But he is…"

"Yes. I know quite well who he is. But it is imperative you see him at once, Edgar. I am most concerned about your health."

"But…I don't think…"

"Stop," Katherine said, placing a gloved hand on her brother's arm. "That is enough."

Helena held her breath. It was unsettling to see the normally lightly voiced Katherine speak with such firm authority.

The clocks in the house began to chime and strike. The little gold flowerpots on the gold pagoda clock began to spin and swirl hypnotically, the jewelled petals

184

opening in time to the musical chimes emitting from its base.

Mr Westcott bowed his head. It was as if all the light and life had been sucked from him.

Katherine's lips twitched as she waited for the clocks to quieten. "Things could be different. I could help you," she eventually said under her breath. "Why will you not accept my help?" Her voice was cajoling, but also had the force of a knife.

Mr Westcott jerked his arm away from his sister's hand, took a handkerchief from his pocket and blew his nose. "There is nothing you can do to help me, Katherine. Evangeline is missing – there has been no word from her for almost a month. My letters and telegrams provide no answers. Don't you see why the clocks must not stop again? Do you not remember?" he said, leaning towards his sister.

Helena squeezed her hands into fists, desperately hoping that Katherine would answer her brother's questions.

But she didn't. Instead, her body stiffened, and a muscle in her jaw twitched. Standing on tiptoes, she gave her brother a fleeting kiss on the cheek. As she turned and swept out of the front door, a single peacock eye drifted from her hat to the floor.

Mr Westcott's gaze lingered on the iridescent feathered eye. A small moan came from his lips. Turning, he disappeared up the stairs, the leaden thumps of his feet echoing through the house.

Helena's father bustled past her, Orbit's cage in his arms. "I shall see you in the morning, my dear. I am fit for nothing but sleep. I shall put Orbit in your room."

Helena gave him a quick nod, her eyes flitting to the peacock-feather eye and the larger than normal blade of light coming from under Mr Westcott's open study door. Had an opportunity just presented itself to search a normally out-of-bounds room for clues to the mysteries of this house?

# CHAPTER 22

# Scrapbook

"I cannot go in there," said Boy, staring at her father's open study door.

"But we may not get this opportunity again, Boy. Perhaps there are clues inside as to why he is so obsessed with the clocks and where the Fox family's things are being kept?" Helena held the soft peacock-feather eye in her palm, pressing it with her thumb. A feather-filled memory was tugging at the edges of her brain but would not arrive.

Boy's nose crinkled. "If Father catches either of us in his study we will be in the most enormous trouble."

"But we already are in the most enormous trouble. You have lost your mother. I could lose my parrot. The Fox family have lost their things and, for reasons we don't understand, your father appears quite…ill," Helena said, slipping the feather into her dress pocket.

Boy leaned back against the wall. "I don't suppose it matters whether I agree or not. You are going in there anyway."

Helena threw her a fleeting smile, then pushed open the door. Boy hovered uncertainly at her heels. The wood-panelled walls stared back at Helena accusingly. The heavy maroon curtains behind Mr Westcott's desk had been drawn. A dying fire glowed in the grate. The room felt cosier than Helena remembered, a place she could imagine sitting and curling up with a book on a wintry day. In front of the fire was an easy chair, a blanket thrown across the arm. Did Mr Westcott sleep in here? She glanced at the family portrait above the fireplace. The two blue-eyed children were close in age to her and Boy. They had a smiley-faced mother and a stern-looking father, but all of them were overshadowed by the huge longcase clock standing behind them. As Helena stared harder at the picture, she saw the faint image of a cherubic moon-face drawn on the small pendulum. It was the same clock Mr Westcott spent so long staring at during the inspections.

"That's my grandmother and grandfather," said Boy walking to the portrait.

"And so they're…your father and Aunt Katherine?" Helena asked, pointing to the children.

Boy nodded. "It's odd seeing them when they were little. Father says he was not close to Aunt Katherine when they were young. But since Mother went away last year, she has not left our sides. She took rooms at the University Arms Hotel in town, as she says she cannot sleep here for the noise of the clocks."

"Was that your grandparents' clock?" Helena asked, still studying the painting.

Boy nodded. "I've never liked it. The face on the pendulum is perfectly horrid. For some reason, Father adores it. Maybe it's because it belonged to his mother. She died when Father and Aunt Katherine were only a little older than us. Their father not long after." She paused. "I sometimes think Father's obsession has something to do with that particular clock. It is rare and quite collectable. It gave him a thirst for obtaining more clocks with mechanisms so fragile they must be kept in good working order at all times."

Helena tore her eyes away from the clock and walked to Mr Westcott's desk. Maybe Boy was right about her father's clock obsession? Sometimes the simplest explanations were the correct ones.

Mr Westcott's dinner tray was pushed to one side, the silver salt cellar upturned. Helena righted it, took a step backwards to open one of the desk drawers. Her boots crunched. Lifting her left foot, she saw a white residue on her heel. She bent, brushed a hand over the floor. *Salt.* Mr Westcott must have spilled it. Brushing the coarse grains from her hands, she opened the largest of the desk drawers and rifled through the papers inside. There were letters to his printing firm, folders of accounts, but nothing to tell them where the Fox family's possessions were being held or anything else for that matter.

"What's this?" Helena asked, pulling out a scrapbook from underneath a file of accounts.

Boy walked over, gave Helena an uncertain look and glanced at the door.

"Go on – open it," urged Helena, passing it to her. Maybe the squirm of guilt niggling at her would lessen if Boy helped to search the study too.

Boy turned to the first page and Helena gasped in

surprise. One of Boy's drawings of the inner workings of a flying machine had been pasted carefully into the book.

*Found outside the skeleton-clock room. 3rd May 1905.*

Boy sucked in a breath, turned a page to another of her drawings of the frame and wings.

*Found pinned to the wall of the third-floor landing. 23rd May 1905.*

Boy's fingers leafed through the pages until she came to the last drawing of the flying machine's rudder.

*Found next to Mother's longcase clock. 10th June 1905.*

The last one had been pasted in just a couple of days before. Boy traced her forefinger over it. Her eyes were watery. She sniffed. "Father does see my drawings," she said. Clutching the scrapbook to her chest, she curled up on the chair by the fire and began studying the book intently.

"Boy," said Helena softly.

"Yes?" Boy murmured, as she leafed through the scrapbook.

"Did you…did you…?" Helena took a deep breath, trying to arrange her words. How should she ask if she had been the one to stop the clocks? She liked Boy, had begun to think of her as a friend. But as much as Helena liked questions, this was a difficult one to ask and she was not at all sure she wanted to know the answer. So maybe it was better not to ask it at all. The clocks had been stopped. The Foxes's things had been taken. Boy was clearly upset at what had happened. Surely the most important thing now was to focus their efforts on returning the Foxes's possessions and ensuring the same thing did not happen to their own.

Boy glanced up. Her happiness at realizing that her father did notice her after all had made her normally sad eyes hazy and full of dreams and possibilities.

"Oh...it's...nothing," Helena said, turning to look through the remainder of the drawers, opening each in turn and finding not a crumb of anything interesting. Helena pulled the peacock-feather eye from her pocket, brushed a finger over the blue, gold and reddish hues. She had seen a side of Katherine tonight she had previously kept hidden, a rather controlling side. She seemed determined to do the best for her brother at all costs. She knew as much about the clock-winding contracts as her brother. Was she helping him to conceal the Foxes's things in the stables? Maybe that was why she had been creeping around there last night, trying not to be seen. Helena needed to get into the stables, but she somehow thought that to be caught poking around in there by Katherine was something she should fear very much indeed.

# CHAPTER 23

# The Stables

The summer night was cool, the rain-tipped grass soaking through Helena's boots and stockings and chilling her toes. There was no pinprick of light, moon or stars marching across the sky to guide her to the stables this time; she could barely see an arm's length in front of her. She slowly skirted past the old paint-peeling bench and continued until she reached the row of trees, which stood in front of the stable door.

Helena stared back at the house, to the thin strips of light at the edges of the drawn curtains. Her eyes moved along the row of windows on the top floor to the very last one – the room of books. The curtains were open and light blazed from the window. After Helena had prised Boy away from the scrapbook, she had taken the stairs two at a time, saying she had to complete more drawings at once for her father. Helena knew that nothing would divert her friend from this task. And it was probably better Boy did not come with her to the stables. If she found the Foxes's things, then it would make her feel terrible for what she had done to the family. The more Helena thought about it, the more sense it made that Boy had been the person to stop the clocks. She knew the whirring clock mechanisms inside and out, would know exactly how to stop them. But if Boy was responsible, then couldn't Helena and her father relax a little? Boy was upset that the Fox family had lost their possessions, and it did not seem at all likely she would stop the clocks for a second time, causing the same thing to happen to Helena and her father.

Taking a deep breath, Helena pushed through the tree belt and crossed the cobbled courtyard to the stable. She grasped the door handle and lifted the latch. It was locked. Her shoulders slumped. It had not occurred to her that she might not be able to get in.

Reaching into her pocket for the candle and the box of matches she had taken from the kitchen, she lit the wick and cupped it in her hands, the orange burn of the flame wavering. She slipped around the side of the stable and walked its perimeter. On the back wall, just above head height there was a small window. The frame was old and crumbling, one of the four glass panes cracked. Helena blew out the candle, jammed it back into her pocket and reached up to give the window a push. It stuttered and grumbled but did not budge. She would need something to stand on to have any hope of getting inside. She glanced around, saw a huddle of old flowerpots. Picking up the largest, she carried it to the window and turned it upside down. A trickle of sweat ran between her shoulder blades. She paused and pushed up her sleeves, heard the hoot of an owl. Standing on the pot, the window was now level with her shoulders. She gave it a firm push. It wobbled. She gave it another push. Helena watched in horror as the entire window frame shuddered, breaking away from the wall and falling back into the stable. *Crash.*

*Oh crumbs.* Helena plucked a splinter of glass from her thumb, sending tiny daggers of pain into her palm. Her heart hammered against her ribs as something soft slinked against her ankles. Swallowing a yelp, she saw a black cat was looking up at her, flicking its tail around her feet. *A sign of bad luck.* Helena forced her breathing to slow, pushed the foolish thought from her head. This would not do. She needed to stay calm and climb through the window. She would worry about how to repair it later.

Hoisting herself up and through the gap in the wall, she landed on the floor the other side with a thud, her feet crunching on broken glass and wood. Dust smarted her eyes and nose and she sneezed. She sucked at her sore thumb, blinked at the gloomy shapes lining both of the long walls. Helena's fingers trembled as she reached into her pocket again for the candle and matches. The match fizzed and hissed, and the soft glow of light threw wobbly shadows. If Katherine appeared now, she would be in deep trouble. She drew in a sharp breath and steadied herself. The stable was like a furniture warehouse, the type she and her mother and father had occasionally visited down by the docks when a new chair, lamp or looking glass was required. A pathway of sorts had been fashioned down the middle of the room and was edged with furniture of all shapes and sizes – wooden tables with intricately carved legs, heavy armoires, chairs stacked upside down on top of each other like a child's puzzle.

Helena's insides folded with disappointment. The furniture in front of her certainly did not match the description Ralph had given her of their things. These items looked expensive, like they belonged inside Mr Westcott's house. Helena tugged at the edge of a dust cloth to reveal a delicately embroidered blue and cream silk chair. Three lamps with matching fabric shades stood on a small card table next to the chairs. She touched the edges of the fabric. It pulled at her memories. She had seen this pattern before. It matched the curtains in the skeleton-clock room. These *were* the furnishings from Mr Westcott's house, things that had been replaced by the clocks. It was as if two giant hands had taken all of the furniture from the house and pressed it together like a concertina in this stable. But if the Foxes's possessions weren't in here, what had Katherine Westcott been looking for the other night?

Wedging the candle between the leg of a card table and a chair, Helena scanned the room. Her eyes landed on a stack of travelling trunks pushed against the wall. The brass locks of the top one were unlatched. Helena frowned, peered at the trunks a little harder. They were the type you would use if you travelled abroad. She thought of Boy's mother, somewhere far away on the other side of the English Channel. She stroked her fingers over the dark-brown leather. The trunks were not dented or pitted, they were smooth and unused. Helena heaved the lid of the top trunk open. Layers of tissue paper fluttered and rustled. She was alone in the dark poking around in Mr Westcott's things. If he found her in here, she and her father would almost certainly be dismissed. They would lose everything. But as Helena tentatively peeled back the layers of tissue paper, she realized she was wrong – these things did *not* belong to Mr Westcott. Neither did they belong to Ralph and his father. They belonged to someone else entirely.

# CHAPTER 24

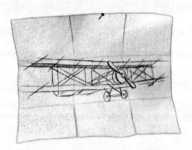

# The Trunk

Velvet trousers. Cream shirts with ruffles. A tweed waistcoat and jacket. Caps and hats and sturdy boots. Unlike the house furnishings, the boy's clothes had been packed haphazardly, in no particular order. Helena thought of Boy in her trousers and boots. These were *her* clothes. Hidden beneath them was a pile of books. She pulled out a copy of *Five Children and It* and laid it to one side. A bolt of sadness rushed through Helena like the wind as she unfolded a pair of Boy's navy velvet trousers. Why did she insist on wearing these clothes when her father and aunt were not around? Was Boy's mother aware of her daughter's strange habits? Re-folding the trousers and picking up the copy of *Five Children and It*, Helena buttoned up her cardigan and stuffed them inside. It was time to confront Boy. There were so many unanswered questions. She really needed to find out exactly what was going on and demand some truths.

The house was quiet when Helena returned, her father's light snores reverberating from behind his closed door. She would tell Stanley about the broken window and offer to pay for it herself in the morning. Something told her she could trust him not to tell Mr Westcott or Katherine about her night-time adventures. Opening the door of the makeshift library room, Helena saw Boy sitting at her desk. She looked up at Helena above the towers of books, the pencil in her hand hovering over a drawing.

"I have something for you," Helena said, slipping into the room and closing the door behind her. She wove her way through the book maze until she reached Boy's desk. She glanced at the paper Boy's pencil was poised over and chewed on her bottom lip. This was not one of Boy's usual technical drawings. It was a convoy of small flying machines in flight over the sea. Small houses dotted the page where the sea joined the land. One was larger than the others and Boy had drawn curtains in its windows, billowing in the wind. Two figures stood in the upstairs window. Boy and her mother?

Helena reached inside her cardigan, pulled out the navy trousers and the book. She shook the trousers out and held them up. "Look. I found these in one of the old stables. Your other clothes are in there too, and the furniture from this house." Helena paused. "Why do you wear these clothes, Boy? You've got such lovely dresses."

Boy dropped her pencil as quick as a lightning strike. She pushed her chair back, her face becoming paler than the paper she had been drawing on, as she stared at the trousers and the book Helena was still clutching.

Helena's arms drooped and the trousers brushed against the floor.

"Please put those things back." Boy's voice was small and cracked.

Helena placed the book on the edge of Boy's desk, held the trousers out to her. "But…these are yours…"

Boy slowly took the trousers from Helena and held them at arm's length as if they might burn her. "You're meddling in things you know nothing about."

Helena took a step forward. How dare she say this; she was just trying to help. "I wasn't meddling, I was looking for the Foxes's things and thought your father might have put them in the stable." A wave of tiredness washed over her.

Boy carefully folded the trousers and put them inside her desk. She lay the book on top and shut the lid.

"I don't understand what's happening in this house," Helena said, unable to keep the impatience from her voice.

Boy dragged in a breath.

"If you tell me, perhaps I can help. And even if I can't help, surely it would be good to talk about it. Mother always used to say, 'better out than in'."

Boy tilted her head and looked at the ceiling, trying not to cry. She parted her lips, as if the words were hovering on her tongue.

Helena held her breath. Would this be the moment she would find out the truth, when everything would become clear?

Boy turned back to the table and picked up her pencil.

Slumping into her seat she began shading in the pictures of the flying machines, the lead of her pencil pressing so hard on the paper they left river-like grooves. "If only he was still here…" she said miserably.

Helena stared at Boy. "He?"

Boy puffed out a small sigh. "Bertie."

Helena drew in a sharp breath. "Who…is Bertie?"

Boy looked utterly miserable. It was as if she was wishing for Psammead, the sand fairy from *Five Children and It* to grant her a wish. *What was Boy wishing for?*

"Tell me, Boy," said Helena, leaning forward. "Tell me the truth and maybe we can put things right."

Boy's eyes were bright and watery. "But what if the truth is horrible? What if nothing can be right ever again?"

"Then it's *especially* important you tell me," whispered Helena reaching out to take her friend's hand and giving it a firm squeeze.

# CHAPTER 25

# October 1904
## Rowing Boat

*The autumn sky was cerulean blue, the reeds at the river's edge burnished with brown and buzzing with insects, as Florence and her older brother Bertie sat on the small bench in the centre of the rowing boat. Florence was clutching her oar tightly, but as usual Bertie was distracted, leaning across his oar to watch the minnows ducking and diving in the sparkling water, which was swollen with rain from an early autumn storm.*

*But the storm had passed, the day was beautiful and their mother lay back in the boat, her hands trailing lazily through the water as her children squabbled and rowed.*

"Hold the oar tighter, Bertie," Florence said through gritted teeth.

"I am holding it," said Bertie, who in fact had loosened his grip even more. Florence was always telling him what to do. He was getting mightily fed up with it. If she had been the eldest he might have understood it, but he was older by ten months and should be the one to dispense advice and guidance to his younger sibling.

"Watch it, we're jolly close to the reeds," said Florence.

"And?" Bertie retorted. "Relax, Florrie. There's no need to be so anxious all the time."

"Don't call me Florrie and I'm not anxious all the time. Only when you're not paying attention…when you're being all dreamy and silly."

"Children," their mother said sleepily. "Do stop squabbling, please. It's so tiresome."

"We can picnic right here," Florence said, turning her oar and heaving with all her might. "I'm not spending another minute in this boat with him."

Their mother sighed, sat up and straightened her bonnet. She pointed to the riverbank, to the branches of a weeping willow dipping into the water. "Yes, well, maybe we need a short spell out of the boat. There is perfect," she said.

The children (well, Florence mostly) steered the boat to

the bank. Florence leaped out and tied the rope to the tree. Her mother picked up the picnic basket and passed it to her.

"Are you coming?" Florence asked Bertie, who had placed his oar down and was leaning over the side and staring into the silky water.

"Can you imagine what it must be like to be a fish? To dart among the reeds and play among the rocks," Bertie said.

Florence snorted. Her brother was so impractical. Father wanted him to take over the family printing firm when he was older, but sometimes Bertie would creep into Florence's room at night and tell her of his plans to study botany and travel to the far reaches of the globe discovering new and exciting species of plant. Father would not be happy with that at all!

Florence helped her mother shake out the picnic blanket, lay out the china and arrange the food under the boughs of the willow, near the fallen trunk of an oak tree. "Bertie never helps," she grumbled, watching him as he leaned over the side of the boat with his fishing net.

Florence's mother leaned across and placed her hand on Florence's. Her gloved palm was cool and calming. "Leave him be. Bertie needs space to dream. It won't be long before his life is not his own."

*Florence didn't entirely understand what her mother meant, but she swallowed the words aching in her throat.* What about me? Don't I need space to dream too?

*Her mother stroked a strand of Florence's hair behind her ear, glanced at the boat, which was bobbing at the river's edge. "I think I might have a little walk along the bank, until Bertie is ready to join us."*

*Florence nodded, watched her mother's parasol puff into the air like a mushroom, and her long skirts trail through the sheep-nibbled grass. She pulled her knees to her chest, rested her head on them and closed her eyes.*

*A fly buzzed by her ear.*

*The breeze rustled the leaves.*

*A splash, a bird diving for fish.*

*The sound of water lapping against the boat.*

*Ducks bustling in the reeds.*

*Then silence as she dozed.*

*"Florence. Florence!" Her mother's raised voice was urgent.*

*Florence opened her eyes. Her mother was running towards her, a gloved finger pointing. Florence watched in fascination as her mother's parasol lifted into the air and landed upside down in the river and bobbed away like a small boat.*

*The boat!*

*Florence turned. The rope mooring the boat to the tree had come untied. She stood up. "Bertie – the rope," she yelled. She stared at the boat, her eyes widening. Bertie was no longer in it. Florence ran to the edge of the bank. She scanned the river, saw the lip of an oar floating away downstream. Her stomach rolled. "Bertie!" she called, cupping her hands to her mouth, her eyes darting up and down the bank.*

*Her brother must have sprung out of the boat, gone for a walk like their mother, or fallen asleep in the straggling, end-of-season daisies. At weekends the river was full of boaters and punters, the bank bustling with walkers. But today was Monday. And it was October. The river was swollen with fast-flowing currents and there was no one else around.*

*"Bertie!" their mother called shrilly. She had waded into the water. Her body racked with shivers as the cold water seeped into her clothes. Letting out a small bird-like cry, she stumbled into the neck-high reeds, which swallowed her whole.*

*Florence ran after her mother, heard her desperate call for help. With a hot burst of horror, she saw her mother heaving a limp Bertie through the reeds. Florence stumbled down the bank, clasped her brother's cold hand in hers. She knew then, with absolute certainty, that life as she knew it had disappeared into the swollen river with Bertie and was unlikely to ever return.*

# CHAPTER 26

# Florence

Boy pressed her lips together, looked at her knees. She was gripping them so tightly her knuckles flashed white.

Helena's head was spinning from the story. Except that it wasn't *just* a story. "Your name isn't Boy. You're Florence."

Boy gave her a limp nod.

"I thought I heard your father call you Boy…but he wasn't talking about you. He was talking about your brother, Bertie. His son, his *boy*."

Boy nodded again.

Helena's head spun. "I think I should call you Florence then – it is the name your mother gave you after all," Helena said softly.

Florence rubbed at an ink mark on her palm, gave Helena a weak nod.

"So after your mother rescued Bertie from the reeds…what happened?" asked Helena.

"We think Bertie dropped an oar and untied the boat to try and retrieve it, but then fell into the river," Florence said in a dull voice. "He must have swallowed a lot of water which made him very sick…and he died. I was sent to stay with Aunt Katherine in London. When we returned to Cambridge, at the end of October, Mother had gone to the south of France. Father said she was fragile…had caught a chill from the river. The doctors said going overseas would help her recover."

"Gosh," Helena said. "How terrible." She bit hard on her lower lip.

*This explained Florence's fear of crossing the river, the alarm she had seen in her eyes.*

"When we returned from my aunt's, Father wasn't like Father any more. He hadn't slept or shaved. The house was in a terrible mess, nothing in its rightful place. All he did was sit in front of Grandmother's clock and stare at it, hour after hour. Then he began to buy more clocks. The servants tried to put the house back together as it was, but Father got very cross and in the end they couldn't bear the upheaval – all the clocks and the chimes and strikes. They all left for other jobs; one by one." Florence picked at the skin edging a thumbnail. "I think maybe it was all my fault."

"But…why?" asked Helena.

"If I had been watching Bertie. If I hadn't been so cross at him for being so dreamy, maybe I would have stayed in the boat, not fallen asleep and he would never have fallen into the river."

"But it was accident," said Helena. "Surely everyone knows that?"

Florence gave a small shrug. "Father refuses to talk about the accident, or Bertie. Sometimes…it feels like he never even existed. So that's why I…began to dress in my brother's clothes, so I didn't forget. But the more I wear Bertie's clothes, the less real I feel."

Helena placed a hand on Florence's arm. She wanted to tell her that she had never met anyone so real in her life before, but did not know how to put it into words. Perhaps for once she didn't need words. Maybe just sitting quietly next to her friend was enough.

"I don't know why the clocks stopped, Helena. And I'm sorry my father took the Foxes's things. I'm sorry he made your father sign a contract too. And I hate how horrid he is to Aunt Katherine. But I think…he's just so sad about Bertie and Mother being gone and I can't put any of that right."

Helena tried to hide the surprise on her face. *Florence hadn't stopped the clocks*.

"I just…wish Mother were here. She would know how to mend things. The longer she is away…the worse Father becomes and the less he seems to notice me," Florence said glumly. "I just wish the house would go back to the way it used to be."

There was a thought about Mr Westcott's odd behaviour at the edges of Helena's brain, like an out-of-reach itch. The thought drifted away.

Florence looked up at Helena. "You said all of our things are in the stables – the furniture too?" Helena nodded. A spark seemed to be growing in Florence, like a newly struck match. "Maybe it would help if Father remembered how it used to be," she said. Still holding Helena's hand, she stood up and pulled her through the maze of books to the window which looked over the back garden. She pointed through the inky darkness towards the stables. "All of the things which should be in this house are out there. All of Bertie's things are out there. Maybe if we get them back, start to make this house look and feel like a house again, Father will remember good things. And remembering good things always makes you feel a little brighter."

Helena thought of the portrait at home in their small living room in London, of her own mother and father and the memories and comfort it brought when she sat with her father and looked at it. "I think that's an excellent idea. Perhaps you should also wear Bertie's clothes in front of your father. It's important he knows how terribly you are missing your brother and the way things used to be. We could bring in a few objects from the stable at a time, rugs, lamps and move the skeleton clocks and return books back to the library shelves. You deserve to have your things back," said Helena. She thought of her own mother, how without Orbit the memory of her would be fading even more quickly. She had to help Florence and her father remember Bertie. "There was a card table in the stables. Did you play games at it with your mother and father and Bertie?"

Florence nodded. "Bertie loved snap. He was quite

ferocious at slamming his cards on the table." Her lips tilted at the happy memory.

"The book I found," Helena said, opening Florence's desk and pulling out the copy of *Five Children and It*. "Was this Bertie's?"

Florence nodded, walked across and took it from her. "He loved to read, always had his nose in a book. Sometimes I stand in the library and squeeze my eyes shut, ignore the ticks of the clocks and imagine I can hear the rustle of pages turning as Bertie reads. I'm going to put that book back in the library where it belongs – along with all of the other books. We can't let Bertie be forgotten. It isn't right, living in a house full of clocks while Bertie's things are outside in a stuffy old stable."

Helena gave her a firm smile. "You're right, Florence. We can't let your father treat you like this. We must take action at once."

# CHAPTER 27

# House Becomes Home

The next evening, Helena's father was doing his usual pre-inspection round of clock maintenance, checking the pendulums were swinging correctly, that the cogs and dials and springs were all in order. Helena was dismayed to see that his usually steady eyes were skittish, his fingers shaky as he checked the clocks. The pressure in this house was devouring him, in the way a shark swallows a fish. As he and Helena entered the skeleton-clock room, he paused. Florence was sitting on her usual chair by the door. She licked a finger and bent forward to rub at a smudge on her boots, then wiped her hands on her (or rather Bertie's) blue velvet trousers.

Helena's father scratched the side of his nose and threw Helena a puzzled glance as he looked into the room. "What…are those?" he asked.

Helena eyed the four clocks, which had been moved along a shelf to make way for a row of leather-bound books. She glanced at the small card table and the blue and cream fabric of the lampshade standing on it. They had placed it to the right of the yawning fireplace near the window. Florence had said that was where it used to stand, when the room had been a place where they sat and talked and played games in front of a roaring fire on chilly evenings.

"Books. A table –" she replied – "oh, and a lamp."

Her father turned. "Yes, I can see that. But… where…did they come from?"

Helena glanced at Florence, who was now leaning forward and feeding Orbit seeds through the bars of his cage. She returned Helena's look and raised her eyebrows.

"Is there a…problem, Father?" Helena asked hesitantly.

Her father's gaze was still fixed on the table and lamp.

"No. It is just…yesterday these objects were not here. And now they are."

Helena scuffed the toe of her right boot on the floorboard. She hated lying to her father, but it was necessary. He would surely put a stop to their plans if he found out about them.

"Is Mr Westcott coming to inspect the clocks today?" Helena asked.

Her words seemed to pull her father from his trance. "Of course." He pulled his pocket watch from his jacket and glanced at it (although quite why, Helena had no idea, as there were twenty perfectly good clock dials in the room he could have looked at).

What would Mr Westcott say when he saw his daughter dressed in Bertie's clothes, the objects returned to the room? Would memories bounce into his head, make him realize how oddly he had been behaving? Maybe he would fold Florence into a fierce hug, promise to forget about the clocks and concentrate on finding his absent wife. Helena crossed her fingers behind her back.

Mr Westcott and his sister swept into the room. "Good evening," Katherine said sweetly. She paused, glanced at Florence, then at the table, lamp and books, then at her brother, a flush creeping onto her cheeks.

Mr Westcott took a step backwards, brought a hand to his mouth.

Helena's father cleared his throat. "Is…everything to your satisfaction, Sir?"

Mr Westcott appeared not to have heard. He walked slowly to Florence, as if he was being reeled into the room on a piece of string against his will. He stood in front of her, his arms limp by his sides. "Florence… why…why are you wearing those…clothes?" His voice was whisper light.

Florence bit on her bottom lip, as she held her father's gaze.

Helena looked at Katherine, whose normally smooth-as-silk brow had furrowed into dainty creases. She felt a burn of indigestion and suddenly wished she hadn't had the second helping of Stanley's sheep's kidneys in gravy at supper. Had she and Florence made a terrible mistake?

The clocks filled the silence with ticks and tocks and clunks and clicks and whirs. Helena willed Florence to speak, to tell her father everything that was troubling her. But it was as if the clocks had stolen her voice, buried it deep within their cogs and springs.

"Go and change into your own clothes immediately," Mr Westcott said under his breath.

Florence sat mutely on her chair, unmoving, her cheeks waxy.

Mr Westcott rubbed his palms over his own cheeks. He closed his eyes for a second, then flicked them open and stared again at his daughter, as if perhaps hoping he would see something – or someone – different. "Florence Westcott…I…I…"

"Come along, darling," said Katherine, helping Florence to her feet. She threw her brother a dark and despairing look. But there was something else in her eyes too, something almost like…gratitude. But what could she possibly be grateful for? She swung Florence round, gripped her by the forearms and leaned close until they were almost nose to nose. "You can dress in any clothes you wish…"

"The books…the card table…who put those in here?" interrupted Mr Westcott, his eyes roaming the room.

Helena held her breath, suddenly wanting to hide.

"Was it you?" Mr Westcott asked, turning to Florence, who was white-faced and arching away from her aunt.

Florence twisted from her aunt's grip, finding her voice at last. "It *was* me, Father. Me and Helena."

"Um…right…well…shall I show you the clocks, Sir?" Helena's father said, throwing Helena an extremely disapproving look. Helena's skin prickled. *Surely if her father knew what had happened to the Fox family he would understand.*

Mr Westcott nodded at Helena's father, swallowed and clasped his hands together. "Yes…yes…the clocks. Show me the clocks," he said breathlessly.

"Come, Florence. Let's seek out Stanley and you can both show me what you have been working on," said Katherine, taking Florence's hand and steering her to the door.

The small nub of attention Mr Westcott had thrown at Florence might not have been the sort of attention she had wanted, but as she was led from the room, Florence had the same determined look in her eye that Helena had seen after they had returned from the Foxes's shop. It was the kind of look that made Helena think Florence would do almost anything to get her father's attention again.

An exotic Persian rug placed in front of the marble fireplace in the parlour.

A bottle-green vase filled with garden blooms, placed on the window ledge in the master bedroom.

Four shelves of books in the library.

Helena felt it in the groans of the water pipes.

The hiss of the electric lamps.

The creak of the stairs.

The ticks of the clocks.

The Westcotts' house was coming alive again, and it approved.

But Mr Westcott did not approve, which only made Florence and Helena more determined to keep on returning things to the house until he did.

# CHAPTER 28

# Five Children and It

"Father is ill," Florence said two days later in the skeleton-clock room, rubbing the back of her neck as if it were sore.

Helena was polishing a complicated brass clock, which had been modelled on Brighton Pavilion. She had wound a cloth around the handle of a tiny pair of tweezers to reach the gaps between the turrets and spires. "What do you mean…ill?" she asked, placing the tweezers down.

Florence sat at Helena's feet, crossed her legs and tapped the mirror on Orbit's cage glumly. The morning sun coming through the window glinted on her boot buckles.

"One, two, pop my shoe, *snicker*, *squawk*, pop goes the weasel," said Orbit, fluffing his feathers.

"Aunt Katherine says Father's head is all jumbled up. I asked her about Mother and she said there was still no news of where she is. I think she has left us. Maybe it is just…too painful for her to return. I do miss her so very much."

Helena's fingers tingled. It had been her idea for Florence to wear her brother's clothes in front of her father, and she had helped bring in the furniture from the stable and return the books to the shelves. If anyone was to blame for Mr Westcott's brain getting more jumbled, she was. "There must be a way we can make things better," she said.

"Aunt Katherine said…I should concentrate on my studies."

Helena frowned. "Your aunt is very keen for you to get a good education."

"She always has been," Florence said. "Even though it was Bertie who received all the attention from Father, but since he's not here…" Her shoulders slumped.

Helena walked to one of the shelves, which was

gradually being repopulated with books, and ran a finger along the spines until she reached the copy of *Five Children and It*. She had enjoyed this book. Had poor Bertie enjoyed it too? She opened the first page.

To Bertie.
Happy Birthday.
From your friend, Terence.

Helena stared at the dedication. She started at the whiplash of a memory.

She passed the book to Florence. "Who is Terence?"

Florence frowned as she read the dedication. "Terence was one of Bertie's best friends."

"A few days ago, a boy was throwing pebbles at your front door. I'm sure your father called him Terence," said Helena, picking up the tweezers again and unwinding the cloth.

"But why would Terence Marchington have been throwing pebbles at our house? He always seemed so quiet, the opposite of his father."

"Terence Marchington?" said Helena, remembering Mr Fox saying that was the name of Mr Westcott's solicitor. "He is the solicitor's son?"

Florence nodded, stood up and returned the book to the shelf, her hand lingering on the spine.

A memory of the telephone conversation she had overheard in Mr Westcott's study the day after they had arrived swept to the forefront of Helena's brain. "I heard your father talking to Mr Marchington on the telephone. He seemed rather cross. He said it was Mr Marchington's final warning and if he failed to follow proper instructions he would dispense with his services."

"But Father and Mr Marchington have always been good friends," said Florence.

Helena's brain whirred as quickly as the tiered clock in the hallway downstairs. "What if…what if Mr Marchington made Terence stop the clocks because he was angry at your father for wanting to part with his services? What if that was why Terence was hanging around the house throwing pebbles too?"

Florence looked doubtful. "But Terence doesn't know anything about clocks."

Helena glanced at the skeleton clock she had been working on. "It doesn't take much to stop a clock – you release the spring and use the winding tool. Terence's father could have showed him how to do that."

"But how would Terence have got into the house? I haven't seen him since Bertie's funeral. I really don't think…"

"He must have come round to play with Bertie," interrupted Helena, pushing away the niggling thought that she could well be grasping at straws. "He must know the house well. Come on, Florence. We should pay Terence Marchington a visit, see what he knows."

"No, Helena. You may not go out today," her father said, handing her a spring for inserting into a tiny jewel-encrusted pocket watch.

Helena threw a dispirited look at Florence.

Florence threw her one back which Helena translated as "try again".

"But I need to go and buy something," Helena said. "For Orbit."

Her father turned to look at her. His eyes were red-rimmed. A knot of guilt tightened Helena's stomach. She had been doing her best to help her father with the clocks, but the work was taking a greater toll on him than she ever could have imagined.

"I must take a train to Huntingdon this afternoon to

collect some rare clock parts. The one shop that could have supplied them in Cambridge, on Rose Crescent, has unfortunately closed – just this past month. Isn't that awful bad luck?"

Helena pushed her hands into her dress pockets and balled them into fists. *Mr Fox's shop.*

"I need you to stay here and work on these springs while I'm gone. You have good and nimble clockmaker's fingers, Helena, and today I need you to use them."

Leaving a list of which clocks she should work on (and a further list of instructions of which clocks to wind should she complete her tasks early), Helena's father bustled from the house and into the hansom cab Stanley had summoned to take him to the station, saying he would be back late that afternoon.

Helena folded her arms and stood by the window, watching the horse pulling her father's carriage clatter away.

"Now what?" said Florence. "I could go and find Terence on my own."

"No," said Helena firmly, picking up the lists of instructions, folding them and placing them in the pocket-watch cabinet. "I want to talk to Terence myself. And I think Ralph should come too. Maybe if Terence sees the hurt that has been caused, he'll be more likely to tell us what he knows."

"But…how can you be certain it was him? And what about the pocket watches?" asked Florence, throwing a nervous glance at Helena's folded instructions.

"We need answers to so many questions, Florence. And we're not going to find them by waiting around here. It will be adding to his work, but maybe Stanley can look after the clocks and we'll make sure we're back well before my father returns, to work on the watches."

Florence flashed her a smile. "If you're sure…"

"Quite sure," said Helena. She thought of Ralph and his family – how they had been short of food the last time they had visited. "I need to fetch something from the kitchens, then I'll collect Orbit and we'll leave at once."

# CHAPTER 29

# Marchington and Sons

Helena found Ralph and his sisters at the vacant shop on Rose Crescent with their mother. Helena pulled Ralph to one side and explained why they wished to pay Terence Marchington a visit. Ralph told them that their situation had worsened and that he and his parents were to enter the workhouse on Mill Road the very next day. His sisters were to be sent to stay with some of his ma's family in Norfolk and at that point he was prepared to do anything that might improve their situation. An ache leaped to Helena's throat. Reaching into her pocket she pulled out some shortbread biscuits she'd taken from the larder and passed them to Ralph. "For your family," she said, and a smile erased some of the sorrow on his face.

As they walked to Marchington solicitors' office, Helena let Ralph carry Orbit in his cloth bag. The boy's watchful gaze hovered over every squawk, nursery rhyme and snicker. She hoped it would provide a small distraction from the terrible predicament he and his family were in. They passed an entrance to a cobbled street backing on to a pub. Two ramshackle, smoke-stained cottages with broken roof tiles and wonky chimneys stood behind the pub; multiple washing lines strung between them seemed to be keeping them upright.

"Ma says nineteen families live in those cottages," said Ralph in a low voice.

Helena's eyes widened. How was it possible that these two sides of Cambridge existed next door to one another; University May Week balls and all of their finery happened less than a mile from this squalid place. They walked on, eventually crossing a wide expanse of grass surrounded on all four sides by buildings. On one side of the green, in front of an imposing-looking hotel, men were playing cricket while spectators watched from a white marquee erected nearby.

"What is this place?" asked Helena. Cyclists hurried along a diagonal path across the grass, heads down and gowns flying behind them like kites.

"A common – it's called Parker's Piece," said Florence. "Aunt Katherine's hotel is just there on the corner. And Marchington's office is to the right of it. Terence and his family live in lodgings above."

"I used to come to Parker's Piece with my grandpa," said Ralph. "He told me of the feast they had here in 1838 to celebrate the coronation of Queen Victoria. Thousands of the poor were invited, even those in workhouses. There was beer and beef and an orchestra. He said it was the best day of his life."

To Helena it had seemed like a rather ordinary public park, but Ralph's memories transformed it into something else entirely, making her realize just how many different sides there were to a place if you rubbed a little below the surface.

Florence soon came to a halt in front of thick iron railings. *Marchington and Sons*, said a polished brass plaque above the green door.

A man with close-set eyes, carrying a briefcase,

bustled out of the door muttering to himself. Helena caught the words "debt and property", as he brushed past them.

Helena curled a hand around the black railing. It was cool against her warm palm. She chewed on her bottom lip. What if Mr Marchington told Mr Westcott they had come to visit? Florence's father would be furious. And he might take out his fury on Helena and her father. But she could not stop moving forward, not when so much was at stake.

"Come on, Helena," said Florence, who had already pushed open the heavy door.

Helena followed, her eyes widening. Dark wood. Everywhere. The floors, the walls, the ceiling. The desk (behind which sat a man with half-moon glasses and hair as dark as the chair he was sitting on). Helena imagined it was like being on a galleon at sea. All that was missing was the jerking of the hull and the slapping of the waves.

"Jeepers," said Ralph, his eyes as wide as saucers.

"Pop goes the weasel," snickered Orbit.

"Can I help you?" the half-moon-glasses man said, peering at Orbit in an alarmed manner.

"We've come to see...Terence Marchington,"

Florence said in a voice as big as she could muster. Helena stood next to Florence, shoulder to shoulder.

The man took off his glasses, leaned forward, his elbows on the desk. "Do you have an appointment?"

"Well no…but…"

"Then I'm afraid you will have to leave. Terence Marchington's diary is full today."

Florence glanced at Helena. "Terence Marchington… has a diary? But he is only thirteen."

The man stared at them. "His diary is full tomorrow as well."

Florence opened her mouth to speak again. The man held up a hand. "And before you ask, it is full the day after that, and every day that follows."

Florence's face fell, and she looked at Helena. What were they to do now?

"Then we'll wait until Terence can see us," said Helena firmly, glancing at a wooden bench along the right wall of Mr Marchington's wood-panelled office. She grabbed Ralph's arm, steered him to the seat and sat down.

Ralph sighed and slumped down next to her.

"*Squawk, snicker*, one two buckle my shoe," chattered Orbit.

"Shush, pretty bird," said Helena, reaching across Ralph to stroke Orbit's head. His beak nipped and snapped at her fingers. "Mother, Mother, Mother," snickered the parrot. Helena's mother's laugh echoed from Orbit's beak around the galleon-like room, ricocheting off the walls and ceiling and sending an odd shudder of pain and pleasure into Helena's gut. Her mother had been kind, would have done everything in her power to help Ralph and his family. And she would do the same.

Florence continued to stand in front of the desk. She folded her arms.

The man sighed heavily, pushed his chair back. "You cannot march in here…with a parrot…demanding to see people who aren't available to be seen."

"It's jolly important," said Florence, placing her hands on the desk.

"Three blind mice, three blind mice, pat-a-cake, twinkle, row, row, row your cake." Orbit wriggled in his bag.

The man's eyes widened.

The front door to the office opened. *Tap-tap-tap-tap*.

Helena turned. *The boy who had been throwing pebbles.* He stood next to a narrow-eyed man who was leaning on a walking stick that was as thin as a cane. The stick tapped again on the floor, once, twice, three times, as his beady eyes skittered across each of them in turn, his lip curling a little when he saw Orbit. Helena swallowed. This must be Mr Marchington, and he did not look at all impressed to see them in his office. She suddenly wondered if she had been a little too hasty deciding to come here, whether she had inadvertently led her friends right into the mouth of a lion's den.

# CHAPTER 30

# Terence

Florence took a step towards Mr Marchington and his son, throwing Helena and Ralph an uncertain glance. "Um…good day, Mr Marchington, Terence. We…we…wanted to know if Terence wanted to come outside and…play for a short while?"

Mr Marchington's eyes narrowed into even smaller slits. His neck jutted forward like a rooster's as he looked her up and down and took in her clothes. "Miss…Florence?" He tapped his walking stick on the floor again, four taps this time. He glanced at Ralph. "The Fox boy," he murmured. He laid his stick across the counter and slowly peeled off his black leather gloves.

"It's them who took away our things," Ralph whispered to Helena, his legs jiggling. "They came the night the clocks stopped and filled up a cart with our possessions."

Helena nodded, placed a steadying hand on his right knee. "And it *is* the boy who threw pebbles at Florence's front door," she whispered back.

"Mr Marchington, Sir…I have told these children that Terence is unavailable for a meeting," said the half-moon-glasses man.

Marchington nodded. "Quite right. Yes, his diary is terribly full I'm afraid. Very busy afternoon ahead assisting me with the ledgers. Well, good day to you, Miss Florence. Send my best to your…father. I do hope he is keeping well?"

"Um…yes…he is well," said Florence.

Mr Marchington shook his head with what seemed to be remorse, pressed his lips together and made his way to the double doors.

Terence's eyes dropped to the floor as he began to follow his father.

"No. Wait." The words burst from Florence's mouth

like water breaking through the wall of a dam. "Please, Mr Marchington. I just want to talk to Terence for a few minutes about...Bertie."

Mr Marchington looked to Terence, to Florence and then back again. He rubbed his chin. Rubbed it some more. "I am very sorry for your family's loss, Miss Florence." He said this with the utmost sincerity and rubbed his chin so hard Helena wondered if he would rub it right off. "Very well. You may speak with Terence for five minutes," he said in a silvery tone which goosebumped Helena's arms. "But make it quick, Terence. We have work to do."

Florence had already steered Terence to the door, had dodged the cyclists and hansom cabs and was leading him across the road to Parker's Piece. Leaning against a tree trunk, she folded her arms and waited for Helena and Ralph to catch up.

"Where are my pa's things?" blurted out Ralph, his fists clenched.

A flush rose up Terence's neck and above his starched shirt collar. "What are you doing here, Florence?" he asked, ignoring Ralph, his brow furrowing. He looked Florence up and down. "Goodness, are those...Bertie's clothes you're wearing?"

"You and Bertie were good friends," said Florence, ignoring his question. "Why throw pebbles at his house – our house?"

Helena thought she detected a wobble in Terence's bottom lip. "Don't know what you're talking about," he said, his voice stiffer than before. He pushed his hands into his pockets, glanced back at his father's office.

"Where are my pa's things?" said Ralph again, taking a step towards Terence.

Helena saw Ralph's anger rising like steam in a kettle and placed a hand on his shoulder.

Terence's lips thinned.

"Please tell us where Ralph's things are," Florence said. "His family have nothing. They will end up in the workhouse eating gruel by the end of tomorrow. Bertie would have wanted you to help us."

"I told you. I don't know anything," Terence said, turning to walk away.

Florence puffed out a breath of air and took a step towards Terence's retreating back. "Don't you remember how Bertie helped you with your reading when you were small? You'd sit in the library, and he'd read to you from his botany books. You said if he ever needed a favour in return…"

Helena swallowed. She had never seen Florence look so…alive, so vital. She was burnt red and orange and all shades in between.

"How can you let a family starve like this?" continued Florence. The words hurled from her mouth like bullets. "You must know something."

Ralph was hopping on the spot. His voice rang out, clear and strong. "Please help us; my sisters are starving hungry. If my pa gets his clockmaker's tools back, he can work again, provide for us all and pay off his debts."

A couple walking a small brown dachshund paused and looked at them.

"Did you stop Mr Westcott's clocks, Terence? Is it something to do with your father? You can tell us," said Helena. "We just want to know what happened."

"Me, stop the clocks?" Terence turned and looked at Helena, his cheeks sallow. "Why would I do that? I am sorry the Fox family lost their things. Very sorry indeed. But I can't help you…or Miss Katherine Westcott… I just…can't." He threw another desperate look at his father's office. The door had opened and Mr Marchington was looking at them, his stick tapping on the step.

Helena stared at him. "What do you mean, you can't help Katherine Westcott?"

Terence's face flushed a dark purple, but his lips were fused shut.

Florence wiped her hands on her trousers, took another step towards Terence. "I'm not going until you've told us where the Fox family's things are," she said, planting her feet firmly on the grass.

Terence began to open his mouth, then clamped it closed again. He turned on his heel and ran off towards his father's office.

Florence stared after him, then sat down on the grass with a thump. "I'm sorry, Ralph. I really thought Terence might help."

Ralph sat beside her, crossed his legs and rested his chin in his hands. "I don't want to be split from my sisters." He turned away, swiped at a tear trickling down his cheek.

Helena's insides squeezed together. She turned to look at the hotel on the corner of Parker's Piece, where Katherine was staying. What had Terence meant, when he'd said he could not help Katherine Westcott? He had seemed quite disturbed when he'd mentioned her, almost as disturbed as Orbit became whenever Florence's aunt ventured near. Helena remembered the commanding nature of Katherine's voice when she spoke to her brother about his health. But if she was so concerned for her family's welfare, should she not have chosen to stay at the house with them? And what *did* she do all day? Helena picked at the grass, flattened the blades in her palm. It seemed there were yet more questions to be answered. But to find out exactly what Katherine Westcott was up to, she would need some help from her new friends.

# CHAPTER 31

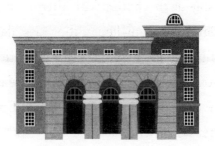

# The University Arms

Helena, Florence and Ralph gazed up at the ivy-fringed Georgian windows of the University Arms Hotel, which were keeping a watchful gaze over Parker's Piece.

"I'm really not sure about this," said Florence, chewing on a thumbnail. "What on earth do you think my aunt could be hiding?" Her earlier bravado with Terence had disappeared. That was only to be expected. Anyone about to break into their aunt's hotel room would feel the same.

"Terence said he could not help Katherine Westcott.

Which must mean she asked him for something," said Helena, stroking Orbit's crown as he swayed restlessly in his bag.

"Why don't we just ask her about it?" said Florence, pulling out her pocket watch. "And look at the time, Helena! Shouldn't we be getting back to the house to work on the watches before your father returns?"

Florence was getting almost as good at asking questions as Helena. And Helena was getting worse at answering them. She chewed on the inside of her cheek, thought again of Orbit's odd behaviour whenever Katherine Westcott approached him; the way she had been creeping around in Mr Westcott's stables at night and encouraging Florence to achieve her ambitions; the way she brought Florence books about architecture and flying machines. Were all of those things yet more examples of a particular strain of eccentricity which had taken a vice-like grip on the Westcott family? Or was it down to something else – something that might help explain the strange goings-on in the house of clocks? Helena did not think she could put any of those things into words that Florence would understand, so she decided it was best to say nothing at all.

"Just remember what we need to do," said Helena

firmly. "First we ask if Miss Westcott is in her hotel room. If she is, we'll have to dash. But if she's out…"

"…You tell the hotel manager you have a very important package for her, and it must be hand delivered to her room – and only by you," piped up Ralph.

Florence scrunched her nose. "Are you sure? It doesn't sound very believable. And anyway, we don't have a package to give her."

"Twinkle, twinkle little star…*snicker*…*squawk*… little star how I wonder…*squawk!*" chattered Orbit.

Helena fed Orbit a few seeds from her pocket and sighed. They had spent a good fifteen minutes trying to agree a plan for how to get into Katherine Westcott's hotel room – which is where Helena hoped some of the answers to her questions lay.

Ralph's idea was for him to distract the hotel manager by fainting, allowing Helena to creep around the back of the counter and take the room key. This plan was quickly squashed when they realized they didn't know which room she was staying in.

Florence's idea was for Helena to march in weeping, saying she was Katherine Westcott's niece and she must leave a personal note for her in her room (because Florence pointed out that if she *herself* went in dressed as a boy, it might confuse the hotel manager and generate more questions than answers).

"Look," said Florence pointing across the road.

The children cowered against the wall of a bookshop. Katherine Westcott had swept out through the hotel doors and the doorman was watching her with admiration. She seemed distracted, pulling out her pocket watch twice as the doorman hailed her a hansom cab. Stuffing her watch back into her coat pocket, she climbed into the cab and it pulled away, the horse depositing a huge pile of dung on the road. The hotel doorman gesticulated after the horse, shook his head and went to fetch a shovel that was leaning against the hotel wall.

"Now," said Ralph, nudging Helena in the side. "While the doorman's not looking."

"Yes…go," urged Florence.

"But…we haven't worked out what I will say," said Helena, her heart beginning to pound.

"You will," said Ralph, nudging her again.

Helena dragged in a deep breath, pulled her shoulders back and straightened her skirts. She passed Orbit to Florence, an idea bubbling at the edges of her brain. She just hoped she could pull it off.

Ralph was right – the doorman was too distracted by the smelly horse dung to notice her slip past into the hotel entrance. The lobby was busy; there were families with trunks and carpet bags sitting on chairs beside potted palms in the small lounge. Two small girls played chase round a pillar, their pigtails flying. Helena strode to the desk where a man was looking at the children and biting his lip, wanting to give them a piece of his mind but not daring to.

"Yes?" he said imperiously to Helena.

"My aunt – Miss Katherine Westcott – has just left the hotel. I missed her by minutes." Helena dabbed at her brow with a handkerchief as if she had been running. "I was supposed to hand over an item for her to take to her room."

The man's face had taken on an unusual sheen at the mention of Miss Westcott's name. "Her niece! Yes, she mentioned she has been spending time with family while staying in Cambridge."

Helena fumbled for the right words. "Oh yes. It has been…lovely having her stay so near to our…home."

"Well now she's taken the lease on that little cottage in Grantchester, she'll be coming to visit you more often I imagine?"

Helena stared at the man dumbly. *Cottage in Grantchester? Whatever was he talking about?* "Um…the item I have to deliver. She gave me express instructions that I must hand it to her directly. Or put it in her room," repeated Helena.

The man smiled and held out a hand. "You can leave the item with me, Miss. I will put it in the hotel safe and give it to her as soon as she returns."

"Oh…I think you misunderstand me," said Helena. "She told me I must take it to her room personally. It is…of a sensitive nature."

The man's curious eyes roamed over Helena's person as if searching the object out. "Well…" he said uncertainly.

"She really has been most complimentary about your…lovely hotel," Helena said, raising her voice over the shrieks of the playing children. "She did mention perhaps taking rooms again at Christmas…while her cottage is being…um…decorated," Helena said, her cheeks feeling warm.

The man tapped his fingers on the desk, then turned and took a key from the hooks behind the desk. It had a large brass engraved tag. *The Granta Suite.* He slid it across the desk. "The porter over there will escort you upstairs. Be sure this key is returned to me within five minutes."

Helena heard a crash behind her. She turned, saw Ralph lying on the floor in a dead faint. She clapped a hand to her mouth and gasped. Then she remembered his plan and smothered a bubbling smile. "Oh, that poor boy over there," said Helena picking up the key and slipping it into her coat pocket.

"Children don't belong in hotels," the man muttered, rushing from behind the counter.

Sending a silent thanks to her friend, Helena walked swiftly to the stairs, passing the porter rushing over to help the hotel manager deal with Ralph, who was now sitting up and groaning and rubbing his head. Ralph caught Helena's eye and gave her quick wink, before emitting another large groan and asking if someone could pass him the potted palm as he was afraid he might be sick.

Helena swallowed another smile and bolted up the stairs.

# CHAPTER 32

# Hatbox

Helena's fingers shook as she slid the key into the lock of Katherine's hotel room. A man in a three-piece suit, puffing on a pipe, nodded to her as he walked past. She nodded in return, smothering a cough in the smoky air. He glanced back over his shoulder, gave her a piercing look as if he knew she was doing something she shouldn't. Helena gave him her brightest and most confident smile. As he turned away, she pushed open the door and stepped inside, closing it behind her.

She blinked in the hazy late-afternoon light streaming through the large windows. The room was furnished well – pretty flowered wallpaper, electric wall lights, and even a small bathroom. On a coffee table lay a variety of ladies' clothing and hat catalogues. Nothing seemed out of order – certainly no files or paperwork in sight that might offer clues as to why Katherine had been asking for Terence's help. Katherine's coats hung on a stand in the corner of the room. Helena ran a hand over the blue coat; she had admired Katherine wearing it one evening to the clock inspection. It was still stained with mud around the hem. She cautiously slipped a hand into the left pocket of the coat. It was empty, aside from a cotton handkerchief with a clutch of embroidered bluebells in one corner. Helena held it to her nose and sniffed. It smelled…not of Katherine's perfume. This was gentler and more familiar, like lavender – her own mother's favourite scent. Helena pushed it back into the coat pocket and checked the other pockets, which were all empty.

A fresh wave of determination washed over Helena as she strode across to a half-open door on the far wall, which led to a bedroom. Hatboxes (five of them) were stacked beneath the window. Behind the hatboxes and next to the bed was a small chest of drawers. On it lay a book. Helena walked over and picked it up. *The*

*Principles of Business.* She wrinkled her nose. That sounded very dull reading. Why would Katherine Westcott have chosen such a title? Helena flicked through it and a piece of paper Katherine had been using as a bookmark fell from the pages to the rug. Helena bent to pick it up, her breath catching in her throat as she read it.

27TH MAY 1905

POST OFFICE TELEGRAPHS

TO: MR E. WESTCOTT, HARDWICK HOUSE,

TRUMPINGTON STREET, CAMBRIDGE.

MY DARLINGS,

I AM ON MY WAY HOME TO ENGLAND AT LAST.

I ARRIVE AT CAMBRIDGE STATION ON 1ST

JUNE AT 17.25 P.M. I VERY MUCH HOPE YOU

WILL BOTH BE THERE TO MEET ME! I CANNOT

WAIT UNTIL WE ARE REUNITED AGAIN.

FONDEST LOVE,

MOTHER

1st June was just over two weeks ago. So that meant Florence's mother was back in England. Helena was certain Florence did not know about this message. But why was Katherine Westcott using it as a bookmark? She must show it to Florence and Ralph at once. Slipping the telegram into her coat pocket, Helena headed for the door, but in her rush to leave, her knee knocked the lid off one of the hatboxes. Bending to straighten it, she saw what was nestling inside the box and clapped a hand to her lips. A dead robin had been fixed to a hat with thin wire, its red breast puffed up, its once soulful black eyes lifeless and staring. Helena's heart hammered against her chest and she felt she might be sick. She was about to replace the lid, when something poking out beneath the hat caught her eye. She gingerly pushed the hat to one side and pulled out an envelope. It was addressed to Miss Westcott at the University Arms Hotel. She pulled out a letter and read:

16th June 1905
Dear Miss Westcott,

Further to my consultation today with your brother, Mr Edgar Westcott, I am writing to confirm that a room has been reserved for him at St Andrews Asylum in Norfolk for a period of time yet to be determined. My report to the Asylum clearly states the difficulties Mr Westcott has been experiencing (obsessive behaviour, paranoia, inability to interact with his remaining child). This has been compounded by his grief at the loss of his only son and heir and the fact that his wife has cut off all communication and her whereabouts is currently unknown. Given the severity of his symptoms, I suggest that he is admitted as soon as the practical arrangements you mentioned to me can be made. I await your further instructions.

Yours sincerely,
R. Barrington
Doctor of Psychiatric Medicine

Helena slipped the letter back into the envelope and pushed it into the hatbox. *Katherine Westcott had made plans to have Florence's father sent to an asylum in Norfolk. What would happen to Florence if he left?* Nausea bubbled in her stomach. Was Florence's father as ill as Dr Barrington thought him to be? Helena's mother had once told her of a lady on a nearby street who, having loudly voiced her opinions on the suffragette movement, had been sent away by her husband to an asylum and never been heard of again.

"I say," said the hotel manager, bursting into the room. "This is really ever so irregular…my…what a magnificent hat," he said, pausing to peer over Helena's shoulder into the hatbox. "That bird is so well preserved, it could almost…be alive."

Bile rose in Helena's throat. "Yes, it could," she murmured, swaying a little as she thrust the room key into the hotel manager's hand and bolted for the door.

The three children walked swiftly back to Trumpington Street in the soft early evening light, heads lowered to the pavement.

"I don't believe it," said Florence, her face taut as a drum. "Why would Aunt Katherine keep that telegram from me? All this time I thought Mother had forgotten us. But if she is back in the country – where is she?"

"There's something else," said Helena, telling her about the letter she had found from Dr Barrington.

"But my father isn't mad," Florence exclaimed. "Aunt Katherine can't send him away – she just can't!

Why hasn't Mother come home? She would put a stop to this right away." Florence pressed her lips together.

Helena adjusted Orbit's bag on her shoulder, a thudding pain in her temples making her wince. Katherine Westcott appeared sweet on the outside, but Helena had sensed that on the inside she was quite complicated, like the inner workings of a clock. But she was kind to Florence, appointing her a tutor to nurture her aspirations and bringing her books. And they were still no closer to finding out why she had wanted Terence Marchington's help. It was all rather confusing and made Helena's head spin and thrum and ache.

Florence's feet ground to a sudden halt. "Look," she said in a breathy voice.

Helena looked up, frowned. Florence's house was on the opposite side of the street. The house was lit up like a Christmas tree, lights illuminating every single window. A few passers-by had stopped to stare at the spectacle. "Imagine being wealthy enough to have electric lights in every room *and* have them on in the daytime," she heard a woman say to her friend.

Helena gulped. Why were the lights on? Her father would be back by now. Had he and Mr Westcott discovered that she had not mended the watches or wound the clocks?

Florence began to run, her feet pounding on the pavement.

Helena grabbed Ralph's hand and chased after her.

"Pop goes the weasel, pop goes the weasel," yelled Orbit in alarm, the cloth bag bumping against Helena's side as she ran.

"Father?" Helena called, as she and Ralph ran through the front door after Florence, letting it slam shut behind them. "Father...I'm sorry..." Helena paused, blinking in the glare of the lights.

Florence was standing at the foot of the stairs, breathing hard. Someone was sitting on the bottom step, hidden from view. Helena pushed past Florence, her pulse leaping in the base of her neck. *Stanley*. His head was in his hands. He glanced up, a little moan coming from his lips.

Helena dropped to her knees, a worm of cold slithering up her back. "Whatever is the matter?" she said.

"What's happened?" asked Florence. "Why are all the lights on?"

Sounds from outside filled the silence. A horse and

cart rumbled along. The ring of bicycle bells. Muffled conversations and laughter from people going about their everyday business.

Helena placed a hand to her neck, tried to soften her breathing. Something was different in the house, aside from the lights and the clearly distraught Stanley. Something was…missing. Passing Orbit to Stanley, she stood up and looked down the hall. At the clocks. The exotic three-tiered pagoda clock with the ferociously fast tick, the one that made her feel agitated and unable to keep still. *It was silent.* The silence spread along the hallway like creaking ice, as Helena ran to the clock and placed her hands on its cool brass exterior, felt for the movement of cogs and wheels and springs.

The.

Clock.

Had.

Stopped.

Stars swam at the edges of Helena's vision. What had she done? *The contract. We will lose our possessions. I will lose Orbit.* She pressed the heels of her palms into her eyes and sank to the floor, every last puff of air expelling from her lungs.

# CHAPTER 33

# Stopped

"No," Helena whispered, her stomach churning like a rough sea. "The clocks can't have stopped…it is impossible."

Florence laid a hand on Helena's shoulder. "Your father wound the gold pagoda clock yesterday. I watched him. Stanley, is this the only one that is not ticking?"

Helena opened her eyes, blinked at the black dots dancing in front of them.

Stanley was shaking his head. "Many of the clocks have stopped. I came back from the university to show Florence a letter from…well…I think it's from the

Wright brothers. When the five o'clock strikes started, I noticed they were quieter than usual. Then I saw some of the clocks had…stopped. I've been running from room to room to check them all."

Orbit wriggled and squirmed in his bag and nipped at Stanley's fingers.

Florence's eyes widened at the letter lying on the sideboard. She ran to it, stared at the foreign-looking postage stamp and picked it up.

The clocks that were still working bonged and chimed the quarter to the hour and Stanley adjusted his grip on Orbit.

Dizziness threatened to swamp Helena. *She was supposed to have been at the house all afternoon – mending and winding watches and clocks. And now they had stopped.* "My father…is he not back yet from Huntingdon?" she asked desperately.

"His train must have been delayed," said Stanley, unhappily, wincing as Orbit pecked at his hands.

"But…we must wind the clocks at once! Mr Westcott will be here to inspect them in fifteen minutes!" cried Helena.

"*Screech, squawk, screech,*" yelled Orbit, wriggling vigorously on Stanley's lap.

Desperation filled every part of Helena's being. "No one must know this has happened."

"But we don't know which clocks have stopped," said Florence, slapping the unopened letter back on the sideboard.

"Helena's right. The clocks must be wound," said Ralph. He glanced at Orbit. "Or Mr Westcott will...he will..."

Thoughts spun around in Helena's head like fireflies in a jar. *She could not let her father return to find all their possessions had been lost. She could not and would not lose Orbit. She knew she didn't have time now, but she would find out who had done this.*

Florence threw a look filled with longing at her letter, then puffed out a small breath. "Well, we had better hurry then. Stanley, you check this floor. Ralph, you check all the clocks on the first floor. Helena and I will do the second and third floors. Wind any clock which has stopped. Now hurry!"

"*Squawk, squawk, screech*. Hickory-dickory." With a lurch, Orbit swooped into the air above their heads.

Helena gasped, stared at the open drawstring bag on Stanley's lap.

"Ooops," Stanley said apologetically, his eyes

widening as Orbit's tail skirted over the top of his head.

"No time, Helena. The windows are closed so he can't escape. Come on!" shouted Florence, grabbing Helena's hand and yanking her towards the stairs.

Orbit flew up the stairs behind them, swerving into the room of longcase clocks, small squawks of delight filling the air. The parrot landed on Florence's chair by the door, stretched his wings and preened his feathers. Helena glanced at him. She ought to put him back in his cage, in case he damaged the clocks. But Florence was right, there was no time. Clicks and ticks and tocks, the gentle whooshes of pendulums hurtled into her eardrums. At least not all of the clocks had ceased working.

"Look – my grandmother's clock has stopped," Florence said breathlessly from across the room. Helena ran to her side. The moon-faced pendulum bob was lifeless, the creepy cherubic eyes glaring at them. Helena swallowed. *Mr Westcott's favourite clock had stopped.*

"Where are the winding keys?" asked Florence.

"Father keeps them on the table over there," said Helena. Florence's eyes followed Helena's pointing finger to the empty table. Helena's legs wobbled. Stopped clocks and missing winding keys. This made no sense. Someone had moved the keys.

"I'll search for them. You go to the carriage-clock room," Florence said. "They are easier to wind."

Helena ran from the room, Orbit's feathers rustling as she brushed past him. The ticks and tocks in the carriage-and-table-clock room were lighter than usual. That could not be a good thing. Helena stood in the centre of the room on a Persian rug brought in from the stable, her hands clenched into fists as she spun round and stared at each clock in turn. Her heart was hammering so hard it was consuming the sounds of the clocks. She placed a hand on her chest, tried to slow her breathing. There! A golden clock with a cupid on top. The second hand wasn't moving.

She strode over to it, her hands shaking as she turned it around and carefully wound the key, once, twice, three times. *Tick-tick-tick-tick-tick.* She had done it. One down, but how many more to go?

One, two, three, four, five, six... She wound each clock in turn, three turns each, putting just enough power in the springs to get them ticking in time for Mr Westcott's inspection. Speaking of which...it was five minutes to six. Five minutes before Mr Westcott would arrive to inspect his clocks. Helena swallowed. She could hear footsteps thundering in the room below and the occasional exclamation from Stanley. "Oh, crikey. Another one which isn't working."

Helena closed her eyes as she wound the eighth and final stopped carriage clock. They must not let Mr Westcott into the room of longcase clocks. Not until they were all ticking again.

Running onto the landing, she leaned over the bannister and called downstairs. "Have you got everything started again?" Stanley did not reply. Helena's nails curled into the wooden bannister until they ached.

The front door banged shut. *Mr Westcott.*

Voices lifted upstairs like a twist of smoke.

Helena held her breath.

Ralph ran lightly up the stairs. "I think I got them all going. What now?" he whispered to Helena, his chest heaving.

"It's no use, I can't find the keys," said Florence, sticking her head round the door, Orbit perching on her shoulder.

"Do you know what a longcase clock winding key looks like?" Helena whispered to Ralph.

Ralph nodded. "Of course."

"Go to our rooms on the top floor. See if you can

find any keys in my father's room – it's the corridor off to the right."

Ralph nodded again and scampered up the next flight of stairs like a rabbit being chased by a hound.

The sound of heavy feet thumping up the stairs came from below.

Florence gave Helena a desperate look. "My father," she said under her breath.

Thoughts rumbled around in Helena's head, like a ball stuck in the wooden maze toy she had received from her parents one Christmas. Each direction her thoughts went resulted in a dead end. *Had the clocks been stopped to hurt her father or Mr Westcott? What will Mr Westcott say? Would her father ever forgive her?*

"I'll stay in the longcase-clock room with Orbit," Florence whispered. "You try and distract my father."

"But…" said Helena. She heard the door to the longcase-clock room click shut behind her and a muffled squawk. She crossed her fingers behind her back and hoped that Ralph could find the missing winding keys, that Orbit stayed quiet, that she hadn't forgotten to wind any of the carriage clocks.

"Good evening, Miss Graham. Is your father ready for the clock inspection?" Mr Westcott said in a low voice, his eyes red-rimmed.

"He has been…delayed," Helena said, her voice wobbling.

Mr Westcott's eyes were piercing, searching Helena for a truth she was not prepared to tell.

"My father said to…continue without him," Helena said, her voice shaking even more. She glanced at the stairs. "Is…Katherine…I mean Miss Westcott not joining you this evening?"

Mr Westcott's lips thinned. "I think my sister has been delayed too." He rubbed his neck. "Now, shall we check these clocks are all in good working order?" He gestured for Helena to enter the room.

Helena placed a trembling hand on the brass doorknob and it rattled.

"Is everything all right, Miss Graham?" Mr Westcott asked, his eyebrows arching as he stared at the doorknob and Helena's shaking hand (which was ignoring all of her internal pleadings to keep still).

"Everything is fine, absolutely tremendous," said Helena gritting her teeth and opening the door, preparing herself for the possibility that her and her father's future was about to take the most terrible turn for the worse.

# CHAPTER 34

# Clock Inspection

Helena stood by the door to the carriage-and-table-clock room, her tongue thick and heavy in her mouth, as if all the moisture had been sucked away by a giant paper straw. Where was Katherine? The clock inspections never took place without her. A small part of her was glad she was not there, for if she had been, Helena felt her lips might have run away with her, giving Katherine a piece of her mind for taking the telegram about Florence's mother, and for hiding from Florence that Mr Westcott was to be admitted to an asylum.

Mr Westcott's hands were clasped behind his back as he examined each clock in turn, his head tilted to the whirring mechanisms.

Helena reached up and loosened the top button on her blouse, but it did nothing to stop the increasing squeezing sensation around her neck.

Mr Westcott picked up a small brass carriage clock Helena had recently wound and placed it to his ear. She held her breath. Had she turned the key enough times? She must have done, for he put it down, his eyes quickly moving on to Sir Isaac Newton's table clock.

Helena could hear Stanley pacing up and down on the landing and the occasional squeak of floorboards. Was that Ralph? Had he found the missing keys? There were no squawks and no singing coming from the longcase-clock room. Florence was somehow keeping Orbit quiet. But for how much longer?

Mr Westcott was two thirds of the way through inspecting the room when he lifted his head and turned. "It is most unusual for your father not to be present for the inspection."

"He…he took a train to Huntingdon. For some clock parts," Helena said, pulling at her collar and glancing at the door.

"Is something the matter, Miss Graham?" Mr Westcott's voice was gentle. His eyes met hers. They were soft, the edges crinkling into a small and encouraging smile. At that moment he did not look ill at all, just incredibly melancholy.

Helena swallowed the dryness in her mouth and shook her head.

Mr Westcott gave a small nod. "I think we are finished in here. Everything is to my satisfaction. Shall we move on to the longcase clocks?"

Helena's hands curled into tight balls as Mr Westcott opened the door and led the way to the longcase-clock room next door. "Um…I…maybe we should wait for my father after all?" she said in a rush, glancing at Stanley, who was waiting for them on the landing, his eyes wide.

Mr Westcott turned. His eyes were still soft, and Helena was sure she could see kindness in them. "I have complete faith in your father, Miss Graham. He is the best clock conservator I have ever employed. No one else has managed to keep these time-pieces in such good working order." He strode towards the door of the longcase-clock room, his hand reaching for the handle.

Stanley leaped in front of him like a leopard, blocking

his path to the door. "I think…there may be a problem downstairs, Mr Westcott. Something I must speak to you about."

Mr Westcott stared at Stanley.

Helena sidled up to Stanley until she too was standing with her back to the door of the longcase-clock room.

"What…sort of problem?" Mr Westcott asked, his eyes narrowing.

"Something…rather private," Stanley said, wiping at the beads of sweat peppering his forehead.

"Very well. After I have inspected the clocks." Mr Westcott's hand reached past Helena to the door handle.

"Wait," Helena said breathlessly.

Mr Westcott's hand dropped to his side. "Whatever is it now?" His voice was laced with mild irritation.

"I think…maybe…you should go downstairs and talk to Stanley. It really is a very…important matter."

Mr Westcott's eyebrows bunched together. "Stanley has told you…his private matter, Miss Graham?"

Helena glanced at Stanley, nodded. "Um…yes. It is really rather…dreadful."

Mr Westcott rubbed his top lip, his eyes questioning.

"I do need to speak with you very urgently, Mr Westcott," Stanley said again.

"Is there perhaps…a reason why you do not wish me to visit the room of longcase clocks tonight?" Mr Westcott asked, his brow furrowing into tiny lines.

"Oh, no. Not at all," said Stanley.

Perhaps a little too earnestly, for Mr Westcott's slim fingers reached past Helena towards the door handle for the second time and twisted it open.

# CHAPTER 35

# Precious Bird

Florence swung round as the door opened.

"Hickory-dickory," squawked Orbit, swooping into the air.

Florence clutched a winding key in her right hand. The clock case in front of her was open, the hood at her feet. The winding key fell from her fingers to the floorboards with a bump.

"Oops," said Ralph in dismay.

Mr Westcott stood mute in the doorway. His eyes flickered to Ralph, to Florence, and finally to Orbit, who was doing great loops around the chandelier

274

swinging from the ceiling. At the sight of Helena, Orbit squawked happily and flew towards her, his wings brushing against Mr Westcott's wan cheeks.

Helena let Orbit settle on her arm, smoothed his wings with a shaking hand. "I...think I should explain," she said.

Florence was staring at her father, her eyes wide. "It isn't Helena's fault," she said in a mouse-like voice.

"Definitely not her fault. Or her father's," said Ralph in an equally small but determined voice.

The sounds coming from the clocks which were still working seemed soulful, as if they mourned the gaps of the lost ticks and swooshes of missing pendulums.

"Perhaps if we can just go downstairs, Mr Westcott..." Stanley said hopefully.

"Quiet!" Mr Westcott's voice was low and commanded attention. His eyes were now fixed on his mother's clock – at the stationary moon-faced pendulum bob. He appeared to be in a trance, his eyes glazed, his face as pale as marble. He walked slowly to the clock and placed his hands on the case, as if willing the pendulum to start again. "This clock has not stopped since..." He paused, his hands dropping from the clock and balling into fists. He pressed his curled fingers into his eyes. "Evangeline…I am so sorry."

"What has this to do with Mother?" Florence asked.
"And Helena's father did not let this happen," she said.

"But…Mr Graham is in sole charge of these clocks.
He promised to keep them ticking…" said Mr Westcott,
dropping his hands and blinking. Colour was flooding
back to his face, mottling it pink.

"And he has," said Helena breathlessly. "He would
never have let them stop."

"Look…look at this pendulum bob." Mr Westcott's
words were so quiet, they were almost inaudible over
the sound of the clocks which had been wound.

Helena's eyes flitted to the moon-faced pendulum
bob. The sneer on its silent painted face seemed
mocking and filled Helena with a deep-seated dread.

"Do you not realize what has happened…what the
consequences will be?" Mr Westcott's words were
louder this time and his whole body began to tremble,
as if he was a rag doll being shaken by a small child.

The room was spinning. Helena's breathing was too
fast, too shallow and a tsunami of dizziness made her
suddenly feel like she was swimming underwater.
"No," she breathed. "No. I truly don't know what the
consequences will be…but…"

"You and your father. You are both responsible for this," Mr Westcott said, interrupting. He walked to a vase Helena had brought in from the stable, filled with globe-like pink peonies from the garden. He caressed a petal with his fingers. "I thought things might be…improving… that there was a chance that…we…" A low moan came from his lips. "Mother. Father. Bertram. Evangeline. No."

Florence's face contorted into a mixture of horror and embarrassment. "Father," she said. Her voice was clear and high, like a leaf blowing on the wind. "Please, Father." She stood in front of him, her hands clasped. "We have found out things…about Aunt Katherine. She…she says you are…ill…she wants you to be admitted to an asylum. But I don't think…"

Mr Westcott's cheeks grew even more mottled, like a fast-spreading nettle rash. "Silence!" he bellowed.

Florence pressed her lips together, shrank back against the wall.

Mr Westcott's eyes blinked furiously as he stared at his daughter, his gaze then moving to Helena and Orbit, who was walking across her shoulders.

"Stop, clock, stop, hickory, dock," chattered Orbit, suddenly taking flight from Helena and landing on the hood of Mr Westcott's mother's clock.

"Oh," murmured Helena.

Florence clutched at Ralph's arm.

"That…that…bird," stuttered Mr Westcott.

"*Squawk*. Pretty bird. Pretty bird," said Orbit. "Mother loves Helena." Helena's mother's laugh tinkled from Orbit's beak sending spears into Helena's heart.

Mr Westcott lurched forward and grabbed at Orbit's feet.

With a screech Orbit took off, swooping around the room in a dizzying circle then landing on Helena's left shoulder.

"Give him to me." Mr Westcott's instruction was a whisper.

Helena reached round and gripped Orbit's feet. He ruffled his feathers and nuzzled her neck.

"Bring the bird to me, now," Mr Westcott repeated.

"Pretty bird, pretty bird," Orbit crowed.

Helena shook her head, planted her feet on the floor and prayed that they would take root and she and Orbit would twist together like a vine, joined for ever.

"Oh, but, Sir…." Stanley squeaked.

"Quiet," Mr Westcott said in a firm voice.

Orbit cowered into Helena's neck, his beady eyes wide. "Bedtime. Time for bed, sleepy head," he muttered.

An earthquake-like shudder was making Helena's legs shake.

"Father...please...no," Florence said desperately.

Mr Westcott strode to Helena and whisked Orbit from her arm.

Orbit squawked in surprise, tried to flap free from Mr Westcott's grip.

All the words in Helena's throat dried up and crumbled into dust, as Mr Westcott turned and strode from the room, Orbit's cries echoing behind him. The thing she had most feared had happened, her precious bird – the last piece of her mother – had been lost. She had gone against her father's wishes and left the clocks unattended while he was out, so the dreadful reality was that she had only herself to blame.

# CHAPTER 36

# Follow Him!

Helena's ears were ringing from the voices, whispers, shouts and sounds of time relentlessly ticking onwards from the working clocks. Her hand still gripped the place where Orbit had been standing just a few minutes before. She closed her eyes. *Mr Westcott had Orbit. She felt so lost and alone. What was Mr Westcott going to do with him?*

Footsteps running down the stairs. More voices, urgent now.

"He's put the parrot in its cage, taken it downstairs and is summoning a hansom cab," cried Stanley.

"Helena. Helena. Please open your eyes," urged Florence.

Tears bunched behind Helena's eyelids. Mr Marchington would probably be along any minute to collect the remainder of their possessions. She had let her father down in the worst way possible. His disappointment would be so hard to bear.

"Please, Helena. You have to come with me," said Florence.

Helena flicked her eyes open.

Florence was kneeling in front of her, her hair wild, her eyes even wilder.

"Orbit," Helena croaked.

"I know. We need to follow Father, get Orbit back," said Florence.

"What do you mean follow him? He's gone." Helena's shoulders slumped. "Orbit will be so frightened."

"I don't think it's a good idea to go chasing after Mr Westcott," said Stanley, his eyes glassy with worry.

"It's the only idea I have," said Florence, leading Helena downstairs and past the stopped clocks, which seemed to stare at her in disbelief.

*But she and her father had not let them stop. That part was not their fault. Someone had deliberately taken the winding keys. Someone was playing the most dreadful game. But why?*

Florence opened the front door and pulled Helena onto the doorstep, Ralph close at their heels.

"Hey." The voice came from the right, at the bottom of the steps. *Terence Marchington.*

Florence dropped Helena's hand and clattered down the steps until she was facing him. "You," she said breathlessly.

Terence looked down, scuffed the toe of his boot on the pavement. He looked up again, thrust something towards Florence.

Florence took a step backwards to avoid him.

"Look…I'm sorry. It's just that…" Terence thrust his hand out again. "Take it," he said.

Something fluttered in his palm. A small piece of paper. Florence reached forward and took it from him.

Helena and Ralph walked down the steps and stood next to Florence. The paper in Florence's hand was jagged at the edges, as if it had been ripped from a ledger.

The possessions of Mr Fox, Watch and Clockmaker
of Rose Crescent.
Stored at 43 Mill Road, Cambridge.

Florence's eyes lit up.

"My pa's things!" Ralph exclaimed, throwing Terence a grateful smile. "I just hope it's not too late."

"Please don't tell my father or Miss Westcott I have given you this. I will get in terrible trouble," said Terence, sniffing.

"What has my aunt got to do with this?" asked Florence sharply.

"Miss Westcott…she also wanted me to give her the address where Mr Fox's things were being kept – she gave me some coins to try and get the information. I was going to help, but I was scared of what my father would do." Terence wiped his nose with the back of his hand. "His walking stick is long and thin and bleeds the backs of my knees." He sniffed again.

*It had been Miss Westcott in the carriage that day – dropping coins into Terence's palm.* Sympathy for the boy weighed down Helena's shoulders.

"The night I came with my father to take the Foxes's things was terrible. Those little girls crying. I was so angry at Mr Westcott and what he had done. I knew if Bertie was still alive, he would have been cross too. I wanted to do something…that would make Mr Westcott as angry as I felt."

"So that's why you threw stones at our house?" said Florence.

Terence nodded.

"Seeing Ralph today…hearing how his ma and pa would end up in the workhouse, I thought better of it. I miss Bertie so much. I know he would have wanted me to help," said Terence. "I found the key to the premises on Mill Road in my father's office. We can go and collect the Fox family's things now." He bit on his bottom lip. "I would also like to apologize for being so beastly to Mr Westcott, after he returns from Grantchester."

Helena's jaw dropped.

"Grantchester – how did you know he was going there?" asked Florence, her face paling.

Terence shrugged. "Heard him tell the hansom cab driver. He had your parrot with him – making a terrible racket it was," he said, nodding at Helena.

Stanley sidled over to speak with Ralph and Terence, to hatch a plan to hire a horse and cart and collect the things from Mill Road as soon as possible.

"Grantchester," said Helena, a memory bursting into her head like a firework. She turned to face Florence. "The hotel manager said…he said…your aunt had taken the lease on a cottage there. Is it far?"

Florence's eyes were wide and owl-like. "It's a village no more than three miles from here. Near to where Bertie's accident happened."

"Then we must go at once. Maybe your father is taking Orbit to your aunt," said Helena, the memory of the decorations on the horrible hats in Katherine Westcott's hotel room looming over her like a dark cloud. She turned, ran a short way down the street, waved frantically at a passing hansom cab. It slowed to the kerbside. Helena didn't wait for the driver to hop down from his seat at the rear, she opened the curtain pulled across the front of the cab herself. "Get in," she shouted to Florence. "We must follow him!"

Florence looked at her uncertainly.

"Come on, Florence. We don't have any time to waste."

Florence climbed in and Helena followed, banging on the cab's trapdoor ceiling to alert the driver above. "To Grantchester," she yelled. The horse set off at a fast trot. Helena peered back towards the house, her fingers tingling as she saw Stanley, Ralph and Terence looking after them open-mouthed.

# CHAPTER 37

# Empty Cage

"I don't understand," Florence said as the carriage bumped them along. "Why would my aunt rent a cottage near to where Bertie...died?"

"There are many questions I should like to ask your aunt," Helena said grimly, hanging on to her seat as the carriage lurched round a bend. They sat in silence, as buildings were eventually replaced by a narrow country lane. The fields on each side were as flat as an iron, the wheat crops bristling in the wind. Helena tapped on the roof of the cab, urged the driver to hurry. She drew in a sharp breath of relief when the first whitewashed cottages of Grantchester village appeared ahead of them. The horse clattered past a pub, the sound of a fiddle and bursts of laughter spilling from the open windows. Was Mr Westcott taking her precious Orbit to his sister? The use of birds for hat decorations was becoming widely frowned upon. Before she had died, Helena's mother had told her of a spirited lecture she had been to in London, given by Emily Williamson. She had helped found The Royal Society for the Protection of Birds, an organization that stood up to horrible fashions and protected birds and their feathers from being used to decorate ladies' clothes and hats. A wave of sickness washed over Helena and she slumped back in her seat. The thought was too terrible to even contemplate – Orbit's beautiful, glimmering feathers attached to one of Miss Westcott's horrid hats.

"Look," said Florence, leaning forward. A lamp on a stationary hansom cab flickered. "Could it be my father's cab?"

Helena banged on the roof once more, yelled for the driver to stop, as Florence fumbled in her pockets for some coins. While Florence paid their driver, Helena jumped down from her seat and looked around for the driver of the other stationary cab. The horse was tied to a tree at the opening to a small lane. Perhaps he had gone to the pub they had just passed? As their own driver pulled away, the sound of horse's hooves receded, leaving nothing but the quiet of a village evening. The odd bedraggled chicken pecking and clucking on the grass verges. The sound of children's voices from inside small thatched cottages. The smell of woodsmoke drifting from chimneys.

Helena gingerly pulled back the heavy curtain at the front of the stationary cab and looked inside. Something glinted on the floor. *The yellow ribbon and tiny gilt mirror Florence had attached to Orbit's cage.* Helena picked them up and squeezed them in her fist. So, Mr Westcott was nearby – which meant her parrot was too. She peered down the unlit lane. Wind rustled the bushes and hedges. They were thick with summer leaves and would make excellent hiding places. A shiver rolled through her.

"Maybe we should go back for Stanley?" Florence whispered, chewing on a thumbnail.

"No. Your father has Orbit. He can't be far from here." Helena began to walk down the lane into the lengthening shadows, a pinch of worry for the disappearance of her own father accelerating her breathing. Florence's breaths came sharp and fast behind her. The lane suddenly narrowed, until there was only room for them to walk in single file. Helena pressed on, gritted her teeth. *Orbit standing in Mother's cupped hands. His beak nibbling at her wedding ring, the gold glinting in the sun that beamed in from the window.* Helena shook her head, let the memories flutter away. Her parrot could not be lost.

"Wait, Helena. This…this path leads to the river," said Florence.

Helena turned and looked at her friend. Florence's lips were thin, her cheeks pallid. "Please, Florence. Please be brave. I won't let anything happen to you."

Florence sucked in a wobbly breath and shook her head. "I…I can't. I haven't been back here since… Bertie…since he…" She paused, looked at the ground.

Helena swallowed. Was this the right thing to be doing – forcing Florence to confront her memories in this way? "Your father is nearby – and Orbit. Please… Florence. I'm scared too. I can't do this on my own. I need your help."

Florence was breathing through her mouth, her breaths raspy. She squeezed her eyes shut for a few seconds and bunched her hands into fists. Flicking her eyes open again, she gave Helena a tentative nod.

Helena threw Florence a thankful smile, then pressed on, pushing past a bramble which snagged her skirts, climbing over a mossy wooden stile and into a field which was fading from green to grey. Something glinting and liquid and wavering ahead of them, like mercury. *The river.*

The squawk when it came was unlike any squawk Helena had ever heard before. It was high and spirited, seemed to be at one with the wind, which sang through the branches of the trees. Orbit! Something else was glinting in the dull evening light, something golden. A lone figure was sitting beside Orbit's empty cage, head in hands. Helena looked at Florence in horror and began to run.

# CHAPTER 38

# Alarm Call

"Father," exclaimed Florence breathlessly.

Mr Westcott was sitting on a fallen tree trunk near the riverbank. His head was tipped to the sky – to Orbit's cries as he swooped and sang.

"*Squawk-squawk-squawk,*" Orbit cawed from up high.

Helena felt as if her heart was bleeding. How were they going to get him down?

"Father," Florence cried again, coming to an abrupt halt a short distance from the river's edge, beside some blush-red poppies shivering in the breeze.

"Florence?" Mr Westcott stood up, his arms limp by

his sides. "Miss Graham? I am so sorry. Your beautiful parrot…"

"You took him," Helena said, white-hot anger boiling inside her veins as she strode towards him. "You were going to give Orbit to your sister and now he's gone, and we'll never get him to come down."

"Why did you take Helena's parrot, Father?" asked Florence, her voice coiled with unhappiness. "It was not her fault that the clocks stopped."

Mr Westcott sat down on the log again with a thump, rubbed at his cheeks. A caterpillar-like shudder rolled across his stooped shoulders. He looked sorrowful and small and lost, not a bit like the mottle-faced man who had swept Orbit off Helena's shoulder. "I am sorry. I was just so angry that the clocks had stopped again and that the bird was flying in the house. I was not going to hurt the creature. I brought him here to the river so I could think. But the cage door opened, and he flew away."

Helena's throat constricted. She glanced at the cage, saw the small padlock was missing. *Her parrot had escaped. Mr Westcott had not set him free.*

"*Squawk-squawk-squawk*," cried Orbit.

Helena stared into the gloaming sky, saw a swooping

shape above. Her fingers tingled with longing to cradle her bird in her hands, feel the affectionate nibbles of his beak.

"But why bring Helena's parrot to the place where Bertie's accident happened?" asked Florence, her voice mingling with the whispers of the river and the rustling reeds.

"I often take a carriage here in the evenings – it is the only place where my thoughts seem less muddled," Mr Westcott said sadly.

A thought spiralled into Helena's head. *The occasions she had seen Mr Westcott climbing into a carriage late at night. He had been coming to visit the place his poor son had drowned.*

Mr Westcott groaned, his chin trembling. "If only Mother's clock hadn't stopped when she died...maybe things would have been different."

Helena frowned, thought of the family portrait in Mr Westcott's study – his mother and father, him and his sister Katherine, standing next to the longcase clock with the moon-faced pendulum bob.

"But what has Grandmother's clock got to do with anything?" asked Florence, giving the river a cautious glance before sidling closer to her father.

Thoughts were spinning in Helena's head, binding together like a spider's web.

*The spilled salt in Mr Westcott's study. His annoyance when Katherine put up her umbrella in the house. His upset at his sister's hat of peacock-feather eyes. His insistence that Orbit should not fly in the house. All of those things were rumoured to bring bad luck.*

How could she not have seen it? Her father had spoken before about people's strange superstitions over watches and clocks. He had once told her of a man who brought a small carriage clock belonging to his cousin into the workshop. The clock had struck twice, then stopped, was thought to be broken. The man had later written to Helena's father, asking him to sell on the clock, saying under no circumstances would he have it in his house. His cousin had died exactly two days after the clock had struck twice – a bad omen and not a coincidence in the man's eyes. Helena's father had laughed, said he had never heard anything so absurd.

Helena's legs wobbled. She plonked down on the grass next to the log. "Your father is superstitious about the clocks stopping, Florence."

"What?" asked Florence incredulously. "Is this true, Father?"

"Yes," said Mr Westcott, giving Helena a sidelong glance. "I was ten when my mother took her last breath. She died five minutes before midnight. Her favourite clock had stopped that same day. It is a well-known superstition that if that happens there will be death in the family. And then…and then…my father died soon after…" His words trailed off to nothing as he stared at the inky river. A burst of silvery laughter from a punt a short way downstream hung in the air. Small coloured lanterns strung around the punt illuminated ladies dressed in white, men in black coat-tails and bow ties. "Look, a parrot," a person from the punt shouted, and a cheer rose into the air like a balloon. *Orbit.* Helena folded her arms around herself to try and quell the shakes rattling her body.

"But how can a stopped clock have any bearing on whether a person's heart stops beating or not? A clock is a mechanical thing. A heart is flesh and blood," said Florence. She sat on the log, shuffling along until she and her father were elbow to elbow.

Mr Westcott sighed a shuddery sigh. "It was a fear my father instilled in me. When he died so soon after my mother – I believed it must be true. And then Bertie died, and my world fell apart all over again, and I became obsessed with the thought that the clocks might stop…I couldn't risk losing anyone else."

Florence glanced up at her father, her eyes wide.

Helena bit hard on the inside of her cheek.

"Your mother was so unwell, so broken when Bertie died. After she left for Europe, I thought the only thing to do was to keep the clocks ticking at all costs," Mr Westcott said, pressing a hand to his lips. "And then she would return, better."

Orbit swooped low to the water then spiralled up into the air, his wings swishing.

Mr Westcott stood up and walked to the river's edge, looked across the water into the thickening dusk, towards the students on the punt. He turned to face Florence, his eyebrows pulling together. "Your mother was due to come home, Florence. I kept it from you and your aunt Katherine – as I was so anxious not to jinx her return. I felt lighter than I had done for a long time, the day I went to meet her at the train station. Except she was not there. When I came home, the clocks had stopped. I thought…it was a sign. That your mother had been taken from me too, just like everyone else I've ever loved. I was so distraught, I instructed Mr Fox to leave immediately. I had to keep the clocks ticking myself, which was not at all good for my nerves, until I appointed Mr Graham. Inserting a clause in his and Mr Fox's contracts that the clocks must not stop seemed imperative. I believed it was the only way to prevent further tragedy and another death…"

"Oh, Father," said Florence, jumping up to take his hands in hers.

The look of earlier caution she had given the river had vanished, replaced with an anguish that made Helena dizzy.

"When I am surrounded by the ticks and tocks and chimes and strikes, I can think of little else but the clocks and my fears for your mother. Yet…now… standing here…it seems nonsensical and slightly… absurd," Mr Westcott said. He clasped Florence's hands tightly. "Aunt Katherine believes I am ill. I think maybe she is right. I am so sorry, Florence."

"But you are not mad, Father," said Florence fiercely. "That's what I was trying to tell you at the house. You are just rather…sad, I think. That Bertie is gone, and Mother is not here."

"Yes…I think I am rather," Mr Westcott said giving Florence's hands a squeeze. "I fear the worst, Florence. I fear your mother may never come home to us."

A small noise flew from Florence's lips and she rested her cheek on her father's chest.

Helena looked away, thinking of the telegram she had found in Katherine's hotel room. Mr Westcott had kept it a secret that his wife was due to return, yet his sister had known about it all along. Maybe now was not the time to tell him this – perhaps Florence should do that later, when things between them had settled a little.

"*Squawk-squawk-squawk*," Orbit cried from the trees on the opposite side of the riverbank. It was an urgent cry – an alarm call.

Helena's thoughts whistled in time with the wind, her senses jangling. She stood up, saw the brush of a green and blue wing looping away on the other side of the river. "No," she cried, her voice reed thin. "Come back!"

Mr Westcott and Florence had turned, were staring at her.

"Orbit's cry – I have heard it before," said Helena. "He is frightened of something."

Florence and Mr Westcott looked at Helena blankly.

"Maybe he has been spooked by a swan, or a moorhen," said Mr Westcott. "I am truly sorry, Miss

Graham. I will do anything you suggest to coax him down."

"I know Orbit. Something is wrong," Helena said, her chin tilted to the sky and Orbit's fading wings.

Florence pulled on her father's hand. "Come on, we must follow him."

"But it's impossible…birds can fly, and we can't," said Mr Westcott.

"Nothing in this world is impossible," said Helena firmly. "I'm going to follow him, even if you don't come with me. I think he's trying to tell us something."

"Impossible," murmured Mr Westcott again.

"Helena's right, Father. Think of my drawings. Think of the Wright brothers!" said Florence.

The near-constant hazy look in Mr Westcott's eyes was clearing.

Helena didn't wait to see what decision he made, there was no time. She turned and began to sprint in the direction of Orbit's cries, as if her life depended on it.

# CHAPTER 39

# The River

The riverbank was slippery from the recent rain, and Helena's boots squelched in the mud, causing her to lose her footing more than once. Florence helped her up and grabbed her hand, as Mr Westcott lurched and slid some distance behind them.

Helena stopped at the water's edge. Face-high reeds and willows blocked them from continuing along the bank.

"*Squawk-squawk-squawk,*" Orbit screeched from up high. Helena saw a flash of blue and green as he swooped above the trees on the other side of the river.

A dull clunking sound was coming from the riverbank. A boat bobbing in the water, tied to a post.

Mr Westcott arrived, panting. "There is no way forward. We must go back and take the carriage."

"No," said Helena. "Look!" Mr Westcott and Florence followed her pointed finger. On the other side of the river was a faint light coming from within a small copse of trees. "Whatever has scared Orbit is over there. We need to get to him."

"But…it's across the water," said Florence.

"It will be fine, Florence. Look – we can use this boat," said Helena.

"We…can't just take someone's boat, Miss Graham," said Mr Westcott incredulously.

"No," Florence said firmly. "I'm absolutely not getting into any boat." She flopped down onto the grass, wiped her nose with the back of a hand.

Helena stared at the riverbank and the post the boat was tied to. This must be bringing back lots of horrid memories for Florence – about the accident and poor Bertie.

Orbit spiralled and sang above the copse. "*Squawk-squawk-squawk.*" The cries appeared to be getting even more urgent. *What could he see from up there?*

"Please, Florence…I know Orbit. He would not behave like this for just any old reason."

Mr Westcott still looked more than a little disbelieving. He scratched his chin as he peered towards the light on the other side of the riverbank. "You said something earlier, Miss Graham…you thought I was taking Orbit to my sister. Why would you say such a thing?"

Helena's fingers fumbled with the rope attaching the rowing boat to the post. "A man at the University Arms Hotel said Miss Westcott had leased a cottage in Grantchester."

"Really…? But why do I know nothing of this?" asked Mr Westcott, his brow creasing.

"What are you doing with the rope, Helena?" Florence interrupted. Her voice was threaded with panic.

"We have to get to the other side of the river, to Orbit," said Helena, jumping into the boat, which rocked and swayed.

"Now, Miss Graham…I really don't think—" said Mr Westcott.

"There is no time for thinking," said Helena. "You will be fine in the boat, Florence. I won't let anything happen to you. Father and I have rowed many times on the Serpentine – in London."

"But rivers are different and dangerous," whispered Florence. "They have currents and reeds and rocks which can take you to places you can't come back from."

Mr Westcott stepped forward and placed a steadying hand on Florence's shoulder.

Helena held out a hand to her friend. "Please come. Remember what you said about impossible things?"

Florence's face was pale in the gloom.

"Well I can't very well let you row over there on your own," sighed Mr Westcott, giving Helena a tense smile. "I somehow sensed when you arrived with that parrot of yours that things would be…different." He stepped into the boat, which bobbed under his weight.

Helena gave him a small smile in return, thrust out her hand again to Florence.

"Come, my dear," said her father, holding out a hand too. "Don't be afraid."

Florence took a tentative step towards them, then stopped and shook her head. "I can't. I just can't," she whispered.

Helena reached over the edge of the boat and held

out both her hands. "Don't let the past stop you from moving forward, Florence."

Mr Westcott gave a small nod. "Miss Graham is right. That is a sound principle to live by."

Helena swallowed. If only she was better at taking her own advice. But her words and Mr Westcott's encouragement seemed to have the desired effect. Florence took another step forward and slowly reached out for Helena and her father. They gripped Florence's elbows, helped her step aboard. They all stood for a second in the dark, the water slapping against the wood, Florence's breathing heavier than the air around them. Loosening her grip on Florence's arm, Helena guided her to sit in the stern of the boat, as low and far from the water as possible. There was a folded blanket under the bench. Helena shook it out and draped it over Florence's trembling knees, checked for both oars, then cast off the rope.

Mr Westcott pushed them away from the bank.

Florence's eyes were shut tight, her head resting on her shaking knees.

Helena sucked in a breath of damp river air as she heaved the oars through the weight of the water.

"*Squawk-squawk-squawk.*"

Florence's eyes sprang open. The boat rocked furiously as she sat up and peered in the direction of Orbit's cries.

Helena's right oar bumped against the riverbed. It was shallow and her arms ached with the effort of keeping the oars steady against the drag of the water. She tipped the right oar back until it was resting upright inside the boat, let it go and rubbed her shoulder.

"Helena," Florence said anxiously, darting forward to grab the oar.

The boat wobbled and swayed, and water swished against the hull.

Florence's face was sallow in the gloom, as if she was suffering from a terrible bout of seasickness. She twisted her body around until she was sitting beside Helena on the narrow bench, their arms nudging. She slid the oar back into the water with a gentle splash.

"You're sure you want to do this?" Helena asked quietly. Florence gave a quick nod, her lips pressed into a thin line.

"That's my girl," said Mr Westcott, leaning forward and giving Florence's knee a squeeze.

"One, two, three, row," said Helena. Their oars were not synchronized, bumping and jolting as the bow of the boat edged a path through the water.

Florence's grip on her oar tightened.

Helena waited for her to pull again, tried to match her rhythm.

Gradually their oars relaxed into a regular swing, leaning forward and pulling back, leaning forward and pulling back.

Helena glanced over her shoulder. They were nearing the other side of the river.

She pulled harder on her oar, Florence matching her stroke for stroke, a blaze of both determination and fear in her eyes.

Helena guided the boat to the mooring point, the bow hitting the muddy bank with a clunk. The noises and smells of a summer evening on a riverbank filled her ears and nose. The slosh of water against wood. The whistle of the breeze. The splash of a river-dwelling mammal as it slipped into the water. The smell of woodsmoke. *Woodsmoke?*

"Look," said Mr Westcott pointing through the trees.

The glow of lights from a small cottage, Orbit screeching and squawking above it.

Helena held the boat steady while Florence leaped out. She swayed a little then sank to the ground as if her body had morphed into liquid. She had been brave to face her fears in such a quiet and determined way.

Helena swallowed. She needed to face her own fears in the same manner. But what if Orbit would not come down?

Tying up the boat, they set off through the small copse of trees blustering in the wind. There was a well-worn muddy path, as if people had passed this way many times before them, tramping on the nettles and pushing aside the tangled brambles.

The glow of the light through the leaves beckoned them forward. The sound of raised voices hit Helena's ears. *Katherine Westcott!*

Helena broke into a run, Florence and Mr Westcott close on her heels. Florence tripped and Helena yanked her to her feet and onwards, until they were standing in a small clearing in front of a white thatched cottage. Two half-moon windows in the cottage's eaves were lit like sleepy cat's eyes. A blade of light from the half-open front door shone onto the doorstep.

"*Squawk-squawk-squawk,*" Orbit cried above the cottage roof.

Helena surged forward, clattered up the shingle path and followed the voices through the door.

"That blasted bird will not stop screeching," shouted Katherine.

"It must have escaped…be someone's pet…" said another, lighter voice. "The poor parrot must be terrified."

Both of them turned at the creak of the door.

Katherine's cheeks were stretched as taut as a sheet pegged to a washing line. She stood beside a woman wearing a floaty white dress edged with lace, her fawn-coloured hair pinned into a loose bun.

Florence blinked as if she was seeing an apparition.

Katherine sucked in a giant breath and reached for the wall to steady herself. Her mouth falling open (in a most unladylike fashion).

"Florence?" The fawn-haired woman said, her voice as light as a nightingale.

Florence grabbed Helena's arm, her nails biting into her skin. Four words carried from the doorstep into the hallway on the whisper of her breath. "Mother? Is that you?"

# Chapter 40

# Reunion

A cacophony of voices in the woodland cottage, louder than all of the ticking clocks in Mr Westcott's house.

"Florence. Oh, my darling girl – you're here! Are those Bertie's clothes you are wearing? Whatever have you done to your hair?" (Florence's mother)

"Oh, Mother! Father and I thought you had forgotten us…" (Florence)

"What…? How…? Oh…" (Katherine)

Florence dissolved so fully into her mother's arms, Helena could not tell where she ended, and her mother began. Her chest ached, and she folded her arms until the pain dulled a little.

"Evangeline?" Mr Westcott whispered from behind.

Helena turned. He was holding onto the doorframe, his face as pale as a piece of Stanley's chalk.

"Edgar," said Florence's mother, her lips breaking into a broad smile. "My love. Are you recovered?" Taking Florence's hand, she brushed past Helena to her husband. The three of them formed a tight huddle.

"Well…this is rather…unexpected," said Katherine, her face flushed. Her brown felt hat wobbled on her head. Around its mustard-yellow sash, emerald-green Bird of Paradise feathers had been artfully arranged. Except it wasn't just the feathers. As Katherine turned, a single yellow eye glared at Helena. The whole bird had been wound around the hat, head, neck, body and feet all on display. Helena swallowed the acidic sickness burning at the back of her throat as she listened to Orbit's warning squawks outside. *Orbit had been distressed by Katherine's hats – by the feathers and stuffed birds. No wonder he protested so whenever she approached him. But her brave bird had led them to this house – had helped bring Florence and her family together again.*

"Katherine," said Mr Westcott, in a voice Helena had

not heard before. It was firm and as calm as the sea on a still day. He pulled away from his wife's embrace. "What is my wife doing here, in Grantchester?"

Katherine pulled back her shoulders and looked her brother straight in the eyes. "I can explain, Edgar…"

"We've been to the hotel," interrupted Helena, her indignation at Katherine's hats still bruising her thoughts. "I found the telegram from Florence's mother that you were using as a bookmark. I saw your hats… you want my parrot!"

Katherine's features tightened. "You have been searching through my things? And whatever do you mean I want your parrot? I like dead birds – not live ones."

"And Helena found a letter from Dr Barrington, saying Father was to be sent to an asylum," said Florence, pulling away from her mother's embrace.

"Telegram? Asylum?" said Florence's mother, her forehead creasing. "Whatever is going on?" With a small shake of her head, Florence's mother steered Katherine through an open door into a room with easy chairs and a fire burning in a grate.

Katherine stood looking out of the window towards the twisting river which had brought the Westcott family so much heartache.

Florence joined her mother on the small sofa, grasping her hands tight.

Mr Westcott stood in front of the fire rubbing his jaw, his eyes locked on to his wife and daughter, as if he would never let either of them stray from his sight ever again.

Helena perched on the arm of a chair, her knees jiggling. As desperate as she was to coax Orbit down, she first needed to learn the reason why Florence's mother was here, why Katherine had taken the telegram and why she had arranged for Florence's father to be sent away.

"Well, Katherine?" said Florence's mother, leaning forward. "Can you explain what is happening here?"

Katherine was mute, tapping a finger against her lips, her eyes glassy.

Florence's mother puffed out an impatient sigh. "Katherine said you were…not yourself, Edgar. She said you thought it best I did not return home immediately. She took the lease on this cottage. In truth I was thankful to be back near the river, close to where Bertie…" She paused, her eyes flooding with tears. "I've been so very weak, and Katherine said Florence was being well looked after and was happy. She was very persuasive."

"But I wasn't in the slightest bit happy," exclaimed Florence. She pulled from her pocket the telegram Helena had found and laid it on her mother's lap. "Helena found this in Aunt Katherine's hotel room. Why were you not at the station when Father went to meet you?"

Mr Westcott took a step forward, picked up the telegram. His face paled as he skimmed the words. "I went to meet you at the station, Evangeline, as you requested. But you were not there. When I returned from the station I searched for this telegram, thinking I must have been mistaken about the arrangements, but it had vanished." He turned to his sister. "You took the telegram from my house, Katherine? Why do such a thing? And what is my wife doing here in this cottage?"

Helena balled her hands into fists on her lap. Florence threw her an anxious glance. Was this the moment they would finally learn the truth?

# CHAPTER 41

# Truth

"It's perfectly simple," said Katherine lightly. "Since Bertie's accident, Edgar has proved himself quite unfit to run the family printing firm, and you, Evangeline, have proved quite incapable of caring for Florence."

"Now hang on a moment…" blurted out Mr Westcott.

The colour slowly drained from Florence's mother's cheeks.

"Wait," said Katherine, holding up a gloved hand. "You want me to explain, so I shall."

Mr Westcott's lips thinned. He nodded for her to continue.

"After Bertie's dreadful accident, I was happy to look after Florence – she is an easy child to care for, not that either of you seemed to notice. It's terrible that poor Bertie is no longer with us, but you have a living, breathing and incredibly intelligent daughter, who to all intents and purposes has been pushed aside by your own self-indulgent grief and insecurities.

"Edgar's superstitions about the clocks stopping are ridiculous. We make our own fates. They are not governed by pieces of metal and cogs and springs. It was a coincidence our mother took her last breath the night her clock stopped, and our father soon after. But Edgar was blinded by his nonsensical beliefs, when in fact he should have considered more obvious explanations."

The idea clapped into Helena's head like a thunderbolt. "It was you! You stopped the moon-faced clock the day your mother died."

Mr Westcott pulled in a sharp breath. "No…no, that cannot be true."

Katherine puffed out a breath. "Yes, Helena is right. I did stop Mother's clock the day she died. But you were too blind to see that the clock stopping and her death were entirely unrelated."

Mr Westcott stumbled to a chair near the fireplace and sank onto it, rubbing his cheeks. "Mother's clock did not stop of its own accord?"

Katherine shook her head. "It was your job to wind Mother's clock when we were children. I thought if I stopped it, you would get into trouble. You had everything, Edgar. The expensive boarding school. Conversations with Father about the printing firm. The month-long trips to the Americas. All the while I was left at home and ignored. We grew up in Cambridge. I would come into town with Nanny and see women going to university lectures, books clutched to their chests, their faces wide with possibilities. Do you remember, I broached the subject with you once – asked if I might apply to study there? You laughed; said I should push such ridiculous thoughts from my head."

Mr Westcott pressed a hand to his mouth and shook his head, as if the words were chiming in his brain and would not settle.

"It was you then…who stopped the clocks again this time," said Helena.

Katherine nodded.

"But Mr and Mrs Fox almost ended up in the workhouse!" said Florence crossly.

A faint blush stole onto her aunt's cheeks. "I am sorry for that. I searched the stables, thinking maybe Edgar had stored the Foxes's possessions in there and I could return them."

*So that was why Katherine was in the stables that night.*

"I spoke with Terence, the solicitor's son. I knew he and Bertie had been good friends. I asked him to try and find out where their possessions were being stored. But he would not tell me anything," said Katherine with a curt sigh.

"But this is…terrible. What have I done? It means my drawing up of the contracts was…foolish and misguided. Mr Marchington did not agree with the clock contract, he has been telephoning daily to try and persuade me to withdraw it. But I refused to listen as I was so intent on trying to prevent another tragedy. The Fox family – I must somehow make it up to them," said Mr Westcott, the slow realization of his actions contorting his features.

"Don't worry, Father," said Florence. "Terence Marchington decided to help us in the end. Stanley will have gone to return the Foxes's possessions as we speak."

Mr Westcott gave his daughter a thin but relieved smile.

Katherine's steely eyes settled on Florence. "Your father is unfit to run the family firm. I have offered my help many times, and each time it has been refused. With Bertie gone, it would not occur to him to allow you to inherit the business when you come of age. The only option was to clear a path for both of us, to find a way I could run the firm and pass it to you at an appropriate time."

Florence gasped in horror.

"But...Katherine...that's preposterous," blustered Mr Westcott, wringing his hands together.

"So that is why you stopped the clocks?" said Helena. "To make Mr Westcott appear quite obsessive and mad, to get him locked up in an asylum so you could take over the family firm?"

"You are almost as clever as my niece," murmured Katherine, giving Helena an approving look. "Edgar did not realize I had seen Evangeline's telegram setting out her plans to return. I sent a telegram back immediately and asked her to come home later than planned, brought her here to the cottage I had rented. When Edgar went to the station thinking Evangeline would be there, I stopped the clocks while he was out and took the telegram, knowing that when he returned his

318

superstitions would cause him to think something dreadful had happened to her. It had the effect of making him quite unsound of mind, as Dr Barrington has confirmed."

"But Father isn't mad," protested Florence, standing up, her eyes flashing. "Rather than helping him, you made his superstitions worse, you made him think he was ill. How could you be so rotten?"

Florence's mother gave a silent and pale-faced nod of agreement and stood up next to her daughter.

"I thought by stopping the clocks this evening, Edgar's descent into his obsessive and irrational behaviour – helped along by Florence's and Helena's actions – would be complete," Katherine said, the words rolling off her tongue as if she took great pleasure in them.

Helena's jaw dropped open.

"Whatever do you mean, 'actions'?" asked Florence.

"Dressing like your brother Bertie and returning the household objects made your father even more unwell. I've arranged for Dr Barrington to take him to the asylum tomorrow. It will do you the world of good, Edgar." She threw her brother a wispy smile.

"Unbelievable," muttered Florence, her eyes aflame.

"Oh, how this saddens me, Katherine," said Mr Westcott quietly.

Katherine turned to look at her brother.

"You are my only sister. I trusted you…thought so highly of you," Mr Westcott said, his eyes filling with tears. "There was no need to be envious. All those years growing up, I wanted us to be close, could never understand why we weren't."

Katherine swallowed, her eyes lowering to the rug. "Well now you do."

Mr Westcott fumbled in his jacket pocket, pulled out a handkerchief and blew his nose.

"This is quite absurd, Katherine," said Evangeline Westcott. "You expect me to let Dr Barrington take Edgar away from us, and for you to take over the business?"

"Why ever not?" said Katherine with a small shrug.

Helena stared at Katherine in amazement. She did not appear the slightest bit sorry. While her misguided actions related to a want of greater opportunities – some of which were difficult (if not impossible) for women to gain – what she had done was cruel and very wrong indeed. Helena thought about Florence and the letter she had sent to the Wright brothers – the books her aunt had bought to encourage her, the tutor she had employed. She thought of Stanley's determination to follow his own path in life, not the one his parents had assumed for him. She thought of the bright-faced women she had seen with their books. She had no doubt that their paths to learning had been difficult too, but she was sure they would not have resorted to such dastardly measures to achieve their ambitions.

Florence's mother was twisting a handkerchief in her hands. It had a bluebell pattern in one corner – the same pattern as the handkerchief Helena had found in Katherine's coat pocket in her hotel room.

"I am quite confounded by your irresponsible behaviour and the hurt you have brought my family, Katherine. At the very time we needed your kindness and understanding," said Mr Westcott, standing between his wife and daughter. He looped his arms around their shoulders and pulled them both close.

A fleeting look of disbelief passed over Katherine's face, as if she could not quite believe that her family did not understand her actions. As Katherine watched Florence and Evangeline sink into Mr Westcott's embrace, Helena thought she saw a hint of regret in her eyes. Katherine rubbed her delicate nose, opened her mouth to speak. *Was she about to apologize?* Then with a small (and slightly sad) shake of her head, she placed a hand to her lips and turned away.

Helena had heard enough. The questions buzzing around in her brain had been answered, just not quite in the way she had expected. She stood up and walked to the door, glancing back at the Westcott family's pale and shocked faces as they absorbed these new truths about each other. She, Florence and Orbit *had* brought the family back together again, but she had a feeling it would take them quite a while to recover and become the family they once were. But in the meantime, her precious bird was still soaring above the treetops. However was she to get him down?

# CHAPTER 42

# Possibilities

Helena sat beside her father on the riverbank under a sunny sky. It was as if solving the mysteries of the house of clocks had helped peel back the clouds and summer was at last rising around them like a fountain. Her feet skimmed the top of the rippling water as she tipped her head, caught a glimpse of a blue and green wing as Orbit flew above a willow tree. "Orbit," she called hoarsely. "Come down. Please come down, lovely bird." The breeze rustled her hair, rushed past her ears. "Orbit," she called again into the silky air, as a copper-winged butterfly fluttered past.

Helena's father placed a gentle hand on her right shoulder. They had been walking along the riverbank all day, her father carrying Orbit's cage as she held up pieces of apple or handfuls of seeds, trying to coax her parrot down. Occasionally he had swooped low enough for his tail feathers to skim the top of her head or her arms, but then he had swooped away again.

Punters on the river had pointed, amused at the parrot singing nursery rhymes in the treetops.

Cyclists had waved and laughed.

Walkers had stood and watched their efforts sympathetically.

When Helena had returned to the house the evening before, with Orbit's empty cage, her father had watched wide-eyed from the doorstep as Evangeline Westcott climbed out of the carriage, followed by Florence and her father. He had witnessed Mr Westcott tell his sister it would be best if she returned to London immediately.

Katherine had bristled at the suggestion, but she had not argued. Before leaving, she'd turned to Florence and Helena. "Keep up with your studies," she had said, high spots of colour rouging her cheeks. "I hope life holds things for you that were never possible for me."

Helena hoped Mr Westcott would be able to forgive

his sister in time, that they would find a way to move forward into a happier future. Although, from the distraught looks on the Westcotts' faces, it seemed it would be a while before that happened.

"It was most alarming," her father had said the previous evening, taking the empty cage from Helena's hands. "My train was delayed, and I arrived back to an empty house…stopped clocks…everyone gone."

Helena had cried then and explained about Orbit, slumping into her father's arms as he soothed her and stroked her hair, promising they would return to the meadows at dawn the following day to try and catch her Blue-fronted Amazon. But they had been at the water meadows at dawn, at midday and soon it would be dusk, and Orbit would still not come down.

"Please come back," Helena cried to the sky again, dinging the mirror on the side of his cage.

Florence had found her mother and Helena was glad about that. But her own mother was gone and would never come back and now the very last part of her had taken to the skies. Her chest ached for the feel of her mother's arms, the throaty gurgle of her laugh as she taught Orbit to speak and sing.

"He is all I have left of Mother. I can't bear to be apart from him," Helena said, her voice breaking.

"Oh, my lovely Helena. Orbit isn't all you have left of Mother. She is in here." Her father tapped at his own chest, over his heart. "She is part of you and always will be."

"But her laugh…I will never hear it again," Helena croaked.

Her father pulled her close, the bristles of his beard catching in her hair. "Mother adored that bird. But Orbit mimicked her, that is all. He is a bird and birds like to fly. Do you remember how Mother would let him out of the cage and he would swoop around the room in circles?"

Helena, gulped back her tears, nodded.

"It was a terrible struggle to get him back into the cage. He loved being free the best."

"But he's a pet," Helena said in a small voice. "Perhaps if we wait here tonight, he'll come down."

"Birds will always return when they are hungry or cold. But do you think he sounds like he wants to come down yet?" Helena's father asked softly. "Perhaps Orbit needs a little adventure of his own."

Helena thought of the small, enclosed cage and Orbit's plucked feathers on the floor. She thought of the poor dead birds on Miss Westcott's hats. Then she looked at the huge never-ending sky, full of the type of possibility a bird may long for. Tears burned at the base of her throat.

Helena's father wiped her damp cheeks with his handkerchief, which smelled of clock oil, metal and wood. "I have been thinking. Perhaps we don't need our own clockmaker's shop. Maybe I have been overly ambitious, blinded by the idea of it. I suppose it stopped me from dwelling too heavily on our own loss." He paused. "I should take a job which allows us to spend more time together. I am sorry, Helena. I fear that since Mother died…I have buried myself in my work and neglected you a little. I am so proud of you, how you have helped me at Mr Westcott's house. Your questioning nature, how you have helped bring that family back together again. You show real aptitude with the clocks, too. I would very much like you to continue to help me…if that would please you?"

Helena gave him a shaky smile through her tears.

Helena's father dropped a kiss on the side of her head. "I think perhaps we should return to the house.

I was talking to Mr Westcott this morning about the clocks. He is wondering about donating them to a good cause – suddenly seems rather keen to get rid of them altogether – particularly his mother's clock. He has asked if I would be interested in helping to establish a museum. It would not bring in the same money as a clockmaker's shop. But maybe we need a fresh start? Perhaps we could talk about it…when things have settled a little."

Helena pulled at a long blade of grass and squashed it into her palm. She did not love the clocks in quite the same fierce way that her father did, but it was true that working on the mechanisms was absorbing in a way that sewing wasn't and Father said she'd demonstrated a talent for it. He'd suggested she had other more surprising talents too – listening and watching and making bold decisions to help piece a broken family back together again. She thought of Katherine and her longing for personal fulfilment and how it had driven her to make terrible decisions. She thought of Florence and her drawing skills and her wide-cheeked smile and "whoop" when she finally opened the letter from the Wright brothers – which invited them to go to London to talk about their flying machine ideas! She thought of

Stanley, who would soon be studying at Cambridge University. Much to his delight, the Westcotts were so grateful at the way Stanley had kept the house running all this time, they had offered him free board and lodgings for as long as he was in Cambridge, as well as a position tutoring Florence at the weekends. There were many ways to live a life and suddenly the impossible did seem more possible after all.

Helena listened to the sound of her father's retreating footsteps rustling over the grass. She sighed, looked to the sky and the scudding clouds. "I'll come back tomorrow, lovely bird," she whispered. "I'll come back every day until you come down." Her words were carried high by the wind to the tops of the trees, into the stirring leaves and creaking branches, where a blue and green parrot sat preening his wings, his beady eyes flashing in the dulling light. A familiar laugh echoed over the trees like a tinkling waterfall and Helena's heart both ached and sang at the same time.

Orbit's head bobbed once, twice, three times, then with a gentle flap of his wings he swooped high into the wide possibility-filled sky, as Helena took a deep breath and stepped towards her own possibility-filled future.

# The AUTHOR

**A. M. Howell** has always been inspired by the stories around her, and how imagination can unlock the secrets of the past. While visiting Moyse's Hall Museum in Bury St Edmunds, Ann-Marie became fascinated by the huge collection of clocks there which all belonged to one man. She began thinking about what an obsessive collector of clocks might be like and after a visit to the Science Museum in London, a story idea began to develop…

A. M. Howell's first novel, *The Garden of Lost Secrets*, was published to great critical acclaim in 2019. A. M. Howell lives in Suffolk with her husband and two sons.

# My inspiration behind writing
## *The House of One Hundred Clocks*

Moyse's Hall Museum in Bury St Edmunds is home to a fine collection of clocks, watches and timepieces, once owned by local collector Frederic Gershom Parkington. I've visited the museum a number of times, often wondering what inspired Gershom Parkington to collect all of these clocks. I began to think there might be a mysterious reason for this, but after doing some research I decided that he just really, really liked clocks! At that point the idea of a story about an obsessive collector of clocks had begun to seed in my head. On a visit to the Science Museum in London we walked around the Clockmakers' Museum, packed full of interesting timepieces (including two featured in the book – one of John Harrison's chronometers and a table clock supposedly owned by Sir Isaac Newton). It is a great place to visit, particularly at midday when the clocks chime and strike. An idea began to develop. What if the obsessive owner of the clocks in my story paid a man and his daughter to keep the clocks ticking and chiming at all costs? And what if these people had something very precious to lose if the clocks did stop?

As I plotted my first draft, I researched different types of clocks and spent a very happy hour at Moyse's Hall Museum with their resident clock winder, who demonstrated how the different longcase clocks were wound, and I even got to wind one myself! I watched YouTube videos of clocks striking to get a feel for the different sounds they make and a friend at work lent me his pocket watch which sat quietly ticking on my desk.

The Edwardian era might not seem a particularly interesting time in which to set a novel – it's the period between 1901 and 1910 during the brief reign of King Edward VII. But in 1905 women were already beginning to fight for their rights, and great inventions and social changes were occurring, including the development of flight, inventions like the vacuum cleaner and the more widespread use of telephones and electricity – all things I've brought into the story.

I wanted the events in this book to take place somewhere that would provide a fitting backdrop to the dramatic social changes occurring in 1905. I had the idea of setting the story in Cambridge as I used to live and work in this beautiful city, with a prestigious university at its heart. But while the university is often the first thing you might think of when Cambridge is mentioned, there is an ordinary working population who live there too. In 1905 there were workhouses for the poor and the two cottages which housed nineteen families mentioned in the book did exist. However, the book is fictional, and Mr Westcott's home, Hardwick House, and the cottage in Grantchester at the end of the book are figments of my own imagination, as are Stanley's and Florence's attempts to help the Wright brothers!

I've always been fascinated by talking birds and the idea of Orbit quickly became an essential part of the plot, a precious memory of Helena's mother that must not be lost. The ending of the story was in my head from the very beginning – a moment of both loss and hope – and I must admit that while writing it I did shed a tear (or two) as I said farewell to my characters, waving them off into their futures, which I hope will be filled with every type of possibility they could have wished for.

The inspiration for this book came from many different places, and I very much hope you've enjoyed reading about it and uncovering the mysteries of *The House of One Hundred Clocks*.

*Ann-Marie Howell*

# Acknowledgements

The first people to see an early idea for this book were Clare Wallace and Lydia Silver at Darley Anderson. Thank you both for your enthusiasm and endless support – and hooray to Lydia for coming up with the wonderful title!

A big thanks to the brilliant team at Usborne, in particular Rebecca Hill and Becky Walker for loving this story and helping to make it the best it could possibly be. Thank you also to the Usborne marketing and publicity team – especially Kat, Mariesa and Fritha for all of your genius ideas on how to promote and publicize this book. The incredible cover art and illustrations made me cry (in a very good way) – thank you Kath Millichope and Saara Katariina Söderlund for your outstanding work.

I'm very grateful to Alex McWhirter at Moyse's Hall Museum in Bury St Edmunds for allowing me to watch the winding of the clocks in the Gershom Parkington collection – and for entrusting me to wind a longcase clock myself! Thank you also to my friend Chris for lending me a pocket watch for inspiration which ticked away as I wrote the first draft.

To all the other writers, authors, book bloggers and promoters, teachers, journalists and booksellers I've met both online and in person – there is not enough space to mention you all here, but I still want to thank each and every one of you from the bottom of my heart for all of your unwavering support and encouragement.

Thank you to my lovely family and friends, especially my husband Jeremy for picking up my terrible typos and grammar and my mum for telling (literally) everyone she meets about my books (one time even persuading a waiter in a café to walk down the road to Waterstones to see my book in the window).

My final thanks are to YOU, lovely reader. By reading this book you've helped make my dream of becoming an author come true and for that I will be forever grateful.

# Usborne Quicklinks

For links to websites where you can find out more about Edwardian life and some of the exciting changes underway at the turn of the century, from women's fight for the right to be educated to new inventions including flying machines and early cars, and see some of the clocks mentioned in the story, go to usborne.com/Quicklinks and type in the title of this book.

At Usborne Quicklinks you can:

- Find out about the fight for women's rights and education
- Watch a video about the Wright brothers' flying machines
- Look at some of the amazing clocks from the book
- Take a video tour of Cambridge and its famous university
- See film footage of Edwardians enjoying days out

Please follow the internet safety guidelines at Usborne Quicklinks. Children should be supervised online.